With many thanks to Mum, Dad and my little Moo and in loving memory of my Lukas, Adam and my Grandads; the guys that gave me the strength and confidence to follow my dreams. I love you all unconditionally xxx

Part One

A Pilot, Policeman and Cookie Monster

I've always found letting go of heartbreak is one of the hardest things; that was until I started writing it down. Rewind to a Friday in May 2012, and that is where this story truly starts…

Love and relationships had never been a strong point of mine. I was either too picky, wanting nothing but a fairytale prince to whisk me off my feet, or I simply ruined it, pushing every decent guy within a mile radius away. It wasn't that I wanted to; I just sucked at being loved. So, yes here I was on this rare sunny Friday, sitting in a local beer garden, having just finished college, still single. There were bananas, policeman, princesses all around me, and then there was me, plain eighteen-year-old Kassia Green dressed as a pilot; a career I'd always wanted to pursue, a dream I'd yet again failed at.

It was our college leaver's day, supposedly the start of a new and exciting chapter of our lives. I however, failed to remain optimistic, knowing my life would carry on consisting of more tragic but stupid, childish failings. It was fair to say most of these would be self-inflicted, thanks to the guard I found myself putting up more and more these days. I know most teenage girls, get their hearts broken from time to time but at the mere age of eighteen I found myself already afraid of love, failing to believe that what they showed on the big screens ever actually happened. Chasing that everlasting fairy-tale had appeared a pretty pointless exercise over my teenage years, so I'd kind of given up on the idea. Some people would call it sad, others lonely, but I, Kassia Green, was quite content with my friends.

My life story so far could probably be listed on my right hand alone. So far it had gone something like this: Year Six SATS (complete success), Year Nine SATS (another hooray! moment), GCSEs (18 of them, all being A*s to B's, so yeh can't complain), Harrison (complete and utter failure) and then there's Adam (a blonde haired and blue eyed wonder yet the biggest heartbreak of all). I think it was fair to say academically I succeeded, love, on the other hand, couldn't be further away if it tried. Unfortunately, I'd accepted it wasn't on the up anytime soon.

The day so far had consisted of silly yet aspiring costumes, many turning up to college half-drunk already, and probably some of the most embarrassing truth or dare games I'd ever been part of. Don't get me wrong, I'm all for answering questions and the odd dance or kiss here or there, but who in their right mind would want to run through the school where you've spent the past seven years, wearing nothing but your undies? Luckily my dignity stayed intact with my worst ordeal being an Irish Jig with Andrew, the nerd that picked his nose all the way through Year 11 chemistry. After as little hand holding as possible, and a thorough scrub, my hands were still as soft as they usually were made better by the thought of never having to see him or his long boney fingers again. It was Callum, the college clown, which drew the short straw even though I'm sure he lapped in the attention. Somehow the thought of everyone staring at him was great for his confidence, not that his ego had grown enough these past seven years. It was the rest of the school I immediately felt sorry for. The thought of poor, innocent year seven's coming out for their break to see nothing but an overweight and spotty eighteen-year-old streaking buildings with nothing but his budgie smugglers on. You would have thought teachers would make it less of a performance, perhaps during a lesson, but no our sixth form was too 'proud' for that. They say proud, I say full on embarrassing, confidence breaking and simply stupid.

After hours of shaming moments and a pre-planned midday finish, most the year found themselves at a nearby pub. Many had opted for the bicycle mode of transport, I however had politely declined and thought a nice, brisk walk in the sunshine was not only a best option, but also the safest. Even when my best friend, Lottie, had suggested I ride her brother's new mountain bike I didn't budge. Honestly I saw no real fascination in these two-wheeled things, seeing them as merely a hazard rather than an enjoyment. Firstly, I wasn't a boy and wheelies and tricks really weren't my thing. "It will be quicker biking" she said, adding "and the helmet will really suit you." The sarcasm that came out of Lottie's mouth sometimes, was truly something. My hatred of any hat, helmet thing you put on your head was clear for all. I had enough problems with finding love without going around with flat, helmet hair. Secondly, my hatred of bikes stemmed way back to when I was twelve.

—

'Car, swerve, cow poo, me, handles bars, face plant'…the rest is self-explanatory. That's pretty much how the story went, one never to be repeated again.

After what seemed about two hours of walking, but realistically was about twenty minutes, I arrived at the small and crowded village pub. Trying to quickly blotch my sweating nose, I followed the loud cheers and banging music around the back into the garden. So, yes, a bike may have certainly be quicker but at least I had arrived without a spec of cow waste on my face. I did, however, know what my Mum had meant when she had pointed to my shoes this morning, " Kass, they are lovely and all but are you sure they are sensible? They are pretty high. Do you not want to borrow my trainers?"

That was the main problem with having the same size feet as my mum. Whenever the 5-inch heels came out, there came another 'sensible', flat option. The problem being, I was about five inches shorter than the rest of group, needing the extra height as to not feel so inadequate. Saying that, trainers sounded pretty great right now, aware that the blisters on my feet were increasingly getting more painful. Luckily I had no intention of leaving this garden anytime soon. Untying the laces and slipping off the heels, I let my feet take relief from the cold, short cut grass. Scanning the garden, I started to strut over to my friends, trying to hide the agony of my feet.

Now I wouldn't say we were the coolest group in the year, just one of the most popular. Having been inseparable since the start of year seven, with only a few minor adjustments, our group had seen barely any upset. We were family. They knew your ups and downs, how to cheer you up but most importantly, when to leave you alone. Confrontation was just something we didn't do.

We knew each other's favourite everything, from one's preferred ice cream flavour to their go to underwear brand. I'm not saying these were the essential must-knows to our friendship success, but it all counted. You could simply say we lived in each other's pockets.

Lottie was the first to spot me, half way through a pitcher of Pimms, no doubt that she'd downed all by herself. That was the thing about Lottie, she ate like a pig, drank pubs until they were dry, but still managed to remain a consistent size 8. I envied her petite body, even more so than her confidence. The first time I saw her, I thought she was one of those Barbie girls, the kind that broke guy's hearts for fun; not that I've ever told her that. I remember the day like yesterday; she was wearing a bright pink skirt, short enough to be a scarf and a bright, neon yellow crop top embellished with a peace slogan. Definitely not someone I thought I'd ever see as a sister. It had been the start of college and she had somehow managed to latch herself onto Harrison. He was quick to ensure me that their friendship was purely platonic and that her addition to our group would be the perfect fit. I couldn't quite see why we needed anyone else but I trusted him nonetheless. There was no awkwardness, no silences and within a few weeks it was like she was part of the stitching, part of the group from the start. We'd been inseparable since, her light-hearted approach to everything being somewhat refreshing.

We'd been together since the start of year seven, building a bond that, at the time, couldn't be broken. Harrison, Nate, Kieran and myself were the remaining originals seeing me through all the ups and downs that my life had to offer. It was no exaggeration; these guys were simply my brothers. Life was unimaginable without them and even the thought would send tremors down my spine. We were a fully-functioning, working unit that needed each other; I just never knew how much.

Harrison was the next to acknowledge me, frantically waving. That certainly wasn't his first pint. It would be evident to anyone, let alone someone that had seen him in a similar state once too often. He was another one that could drink for England.

"Kass, c'mon. You've already missed out on the first round, sit down, these are on me."

There was that smile, the same smile I fell in love all those years ago. This was the same Harrison that was on my list of tragic, romantic failures. He was my best friend, the one I was closest too, my first point of call and my go to man. The relationship we had was so genuine, both having those extra feelings, yet neither of us taking to plunge to admit them. I guess in a way this summed me up to a 'T', always too scared to put my heart on the line. It was times like these where I felt I loved him more, his upbeat personality finding an extra gear with the summer rays. His eyes would light up, the smile got bigger and his foghorn of a voice managed to find another level. This was him at his happiest. I'd often thought of Harrison and I as an item but never saw a happy or sad outcome. It was a hard one to read. Either way Harrison was far too important so to have him in my life was all that mattered; romantically or brotherly was still to be decided.

I acknowledged him back with a return smile, still holding my favourite black Irregular Choice heels. "Wait for me, I'll come with you" I replied, knowing full well his round meant a pitcher each for the girls and a pint or two each for the guys. Luckily our group was small, still this guy had more money than sense sometimes but I suppose this was a cause for celebration. We were college leavers, university goers, and a group now separating to five different cities. However, if it was up to Harrison, Harry for short, there was very little chance of any of us leaving this pub sober. The thought of not seeing these people on a daily basis was sad, yet I knew nothing would break us, not even the daunting figure of a hundred miles. We'd be fine, we had to be.

After throwing my heels at Lottie with a brisk "Hey guys" to the rest, I followed Harry into the small and crowded bar. Consisting mainly of Brookhill Academy college leavers, the two girls behind the bar clearly didn't know what had hit them. These girls couldn't have been far out of college themselves, one clearly being more confident than the other. The taller, brunette girl was leaning effortlessly on the bar chatting away, flirting was probably more accurate, to Callum on the far side of the bar. She obviously lacked no confidence and would clearly do as little work as possible. It was the other girl I felt sorry for; scurrying around, pouring pints, pitchers and the occasional cocktail for the know it all, posh girls of the year. Hardly being able to make eye contact with anyone, she kept her head down, efficiently trying to keep the queues at bay. With our arrival, her shift had become twice as long.

The pub, know to locals as The Baggers, was an old Victorian pub, the type to have all its original structures, dark lighting and the same entertainment that never changed. It's interior was decked out in a deep red, the warm and inviting low-level ceiling giving it more spirit than it first looked. It was quite obviously an old man's pub, the kind where the same regulars turned up every day at the same time. They'd drink the same bitter, the same number of pints then walk off home to a nice home-cooked meal. They had they're routine figured out, and even if it did lack spontaneity, you had to admire them. The odd local band would come and play a few Oasis songs, with an acoustic guitar, on a Sunday night but apart from that the ambience pretty much would stay the same. Well that was until, a hundred eighteen year olds rocked up. The majority of retirees had most probably left at the first sight of us, with only a few still jotted around the place, hidden away in the quite coves of the place.

Harry and I spoke as usual, no awkward silences, just non-stop laughing with the odd bit of flirting thrown in. That was our relationship summed up, we were both natural flirts – me using my fiery red hair and so called amazing eyes as my pulling point, Harry simply being louder than anyone else, using those cheesy, blockbuster kind of pick up lines. Others would often cringe, I just bantered back. Bless him, he really did mean no harm it's just no one got him like I did. Looking at him now, I think that was our problem – we really were too close to each other, no other person would dare get in the middle of it. Maybe that was why we were both standing here single. Yes I was scared of love, but was this merely a case of me not wanting to hurt or leave my best friend behind? We were so used to doing everything together, needing one another's opinion or reassurance before making any major decisions, and who to love was certainly one of those. He'd been my protector for so many years, I honestly just didn't know how to a take a leap of faith without him holding my hand. Harry was the only other guy, apart from my own father, that I could rely on – when things got tough, he was there, simply saying "Someone cares Kass, I've always got you're back." It was the only comfort any girl needed.

We waited our turn patiently, still engrossed in conversation about anything, totally oblivious to what was going on around us. That was until no one other than Callum dropped a whole tray of Carlings all over himself, the floor and all over the back of Lauren and Jack. Knowing him, he was probably still trying to show off to the barmaid. With very little success, he now stood in the middle of a packed bar looking even more of an idiot than he did in those ridiculous, gold, spandex pants he wore earlier. Over the cries of "Idiot" and shame pointing, he stood there covered in about twenty pounds worth of alcohol. Beside him, Lauren and Jack were crouched down looking mortified. Those two were always stuck together, probably down to the fact they struggled to find anyone else to befriend. On paper, they were very much like chalk and cheese yet the sight of them together was one of happiness. They may have been different but their friendship was a mirror image of mine and Harry's; unquestionable, undeniable and most notably of all, unbreakable. Over the requested 90's tunes playlist, Jack could be heard muttering under his breath quite clearly frustrated by the somewhat class clown. Callum really was as immature as it got and thankfully he was off to Edinburgh, many miles away from my preferred university in Manchester.

I'd never really spoken to Jack, Lauren really not being my cup of tea with her goth, black and piercing appearance, but even I couldn't help feeling the disappointment and embarrassment he was feeling. He was one of those guys that kept himself very much to himself, not having a bad word to say about anyone yet always seeming to be on the receiving end of everyone else's jokes. Like in year nine, when some year tens thought it would be hilarious to put super glue on several chairs in the cafeteria, leaving poor Jack with a plastic chair stuck to his bottom until he could get his mum to bring him in new trousers. Even though funny at the time, it was horrible to now think of all the bad luck he had encountered, yet he still somehow found the strength to carry on – something I admired. His cookie monster costume was now completely drenched, looking far from the friendly, childhood, animated character we all knew. What this had to do with an aspiring occupation, I'll never know but it was an impressive costume to say the least.

Harry had reached the bar and had unsurprisingly managed to get conversation and eye contact with the shy barmaid. That was another thing about Harry; he seemed to have the knack of getting chat from even the quietest people. He had a presence that everyone bounced off, bringing a little bit of happiness to even the dullest of moments. Whilst I watched the other barmaid do some actual labour, busily mopping the lager splattered floor, Harry ordered the drinks in his usual proud and assertive manner. From the bar, loud hoots kept catching my attention, Harry's usual flirting techniques being in full swing. People would often ask 'does it not hurt you to see him like that?' Truth is, it didn't. I wanted him happy more than anyone else and that's all that mattered. I knew how he felt, nothing would take that away. Poor girl didn't quite realize this was just Harry being friendly but it seemed to have made her day. I couldn't help but smile to myself, my Harry being selfless yet again. There was nothing not to love about this man. He was caring yet daring, radiated confidence and surprisingly looked boyishly handsome in his policeman uniform. I'd often thought about telling him how I felt, but now I really was struggling to keep it to myself. I needed a distraction, and quick, before making a decision I truly regretted.

Tattoo Man

Harry and I pushed our way back through the crowds of people to our sunny spot in the ever busying beer garden, him balancing pitchers like it was a circus act, me wearingly juggling pints knowing the value of the liquid inside. By the time we'd reached the rest of the group my mind was still flicking back to the fantasies of Harry and myself. I kept telling myself it was stupid yet my mind kept questioning 'what if?' Aware of conversation going on around me, I tried my hardest to concentrate on the here and now. That was until I saw him; saw tattoo man.

There were three of them; all brown haired and wearing shades that belonged in the 70's. They couldn't have been more than five years my senior yet appeared to carry an established but mysterious edge. Tight, white t-shirts showed off their prominent arm muscles, with different, brightly coloured chinos of blue, red and green, and smart brown shoes making up the rest of their outfit. Together they looked like a boy band, clearly coordinating their clothes before they met up. At first it was the slightly taller one of the three, standing on the right, which caught my attention. He had a short, sleek hair cut, one of those small nose rings and what looked like an angel wing tattoo on his left hand. He was simply gorgeous. I wasn't normally a fan of tattoos for I had a great fear of needles, but his seemed sensitive probably representing a sorrow story. It wasn't until the middle guy appeared to glance my way that I changed fan base.

He had broad shoulders, quite clearly tanned well (unlike my English rose skin) and had arms covered in intricate, black tattoos. He wore his skin tight, striking, red chinos extremely well, quite clearly outlining a rather generous male package. This guy carried no shame, and so he shouldn't. I doubt he lacked female attention. He carried a distinctive swagger, often ruffling his already messy bed hair. Then he smiled, and with one action his entire beauty became appreciated. It was seductive, a smile that could kill, drawing you in without you even noticing. Without even knowing his morning beauty regime, you could tell this guy needed very little effort, holding an instant summer glow. If I thought Harry's smile was something, this was love. OK, so maybe not one of those cliché fairytale love at first sight scenarios but it was definitely something.

It was like a scene out the movies; three attractive sex gods walking into a crowded place automatically taking everyone's attention. It was clearly a movie that just starred them, and myself - everyone else being too caught up in a game of beer pong and dance offs. Everyone had now left our bench, leaving me looking alone and dazed.
"Kass, Kass, Kassia Green! Are you listening?" I'd obviously been zoned out for longer than I thought. No one ever used my full name apart from my mum (normally when she wanted something doing) or my dad, saying, "it was the name I was born with so the name he was using." I blinked and turned around to see Harry and Lottie looking at me rather bemused.

"Hey guys, whats up?" I said, cheerily trying to sound with it. Lottie still looking concerned, replied "you can't be drunk already Kass, you've had about one sip of that Pimms," pointing to the only full pitcher on the table, "the boys are worrying, you haven't said a word to them since you arrived."

"Sorry, I was just daydreaming, you know me. I'll finish this drink then I'll be over." Downing my warm, already poured glass, I followed the guys over to where the Nate and Kieran were deep in conversation. Daydreaming was clearly all it was, all it could be, for the next time I glanced over to the spot where the men were standing they were gone, like they'd never been there in the first place. Who could blame them? Being surrounded by a whole load of rowdy, half drunken college leavers probably wasn't their idea of a fun Friday afternoon.

Before reaching the rest of the group, Nate had been bullied into a game of beer pong. He'd never been one for competition but surprisingly he seemed to be winning. I think beginners luck was obvious. Seeing me, he downed another pint before stumbling over to me. His drunkenness had been less obvious when he was standing at the table, tossing balls into cups, but now he struggled to stand. Reaching me, he put his arms out mumbling something that sounded like "Kass, I thought you'd forgotten me," even though it sounded nothing of the sort. I managed to save him from falling head first into the quaint but pretty borders that outlined the garden, before replying him "never." That was true. Nate was the baby of the group, even though the eldest.

Being a September baby he was expected to be the mature one, the sensible one yet he was the quiet one, the one that liked reassurance. He never needed much attention but liked it fully when he got it. The sad fact is that he never used to be like this. It wasn't until year nine where Jessica, the school's next top model (yeh like hell she was) broke his heart. We think it's us girls that get hurt the most, with guys being the least sensitive and heartless people on the planet, but in front of me hung a guy so broken he'd give some of us girls a run for our money. Since then he'd been vulnerable, not letting himself trust another woman again. Looking at him now, actually letting his guard down for once, made all those silent hugs and teary conversations worth it. I never did like that Jessica but now I found myself pitying her, she really did lose one heck of a Mr Perfect. Yes, he may be the most drunk here, slurring every word he said, not knowing when enough was enough but he genuinely seemed happy. At least the hangover wouldn't kick in until tomorrow.

I didn't mind, but honestly could these guys not act their age for once. You would have thought they were fifteen not adults about to be heading off to university. What they'd do without me being by their side to carry them home after a few too many or advise them on what was a good pulling outfit would be an interesting one to watch. Harry would often think red chinos (he didn't pull them off like tattoo man did) and an orange shirt was a perfect combination. He would often act offended and disgusted with my silent, disapproving shake of the head, simply sulking "but it's my favourite." He never had got the dating game, my Harry, something I secretly enjoyed watching. It would take one special girl to take him away. I know that sounded selfish but the thought of letting him go sacred me to death. Kieran, on the other hand, seemed to just try too hard; wearing a tie or dickey bow out clubbing was just looking desperate. He'd often look out of place, like a boring, old businessman within a dance floor of legless young adults, a picture that just doesn't make sense. Making it my last task before we all set off in different directions, these, now men, would learn the art of romance and love if it was the last thing I did.

Whilst harbouring confusing feelings towards Harry, my effort would mainly be shared between the others. They both deserved love, we all did but what did I really know about it? I knew the lies they told you on the big screens and in the heart-warming novels that lined my shelves. They did have a prince charming in though so I guess it was a start; at the very least they'd learn a few things about what makes a dapper outfit.

Snapping back out of yet another daydream, I was still holding Nate, who was now being violently sick over the pansies and neatly primed rose bush. At least he'd had a good afternoon, I thought, even though it was only half three. Not being able to concentrate, I found myself looking for tattoo man again. There had been something about his presence that had changed my whole perspective of men. From first impressions, he'd seemed sensitive, his tattoos only showing his creative and passionate side. His muscles seemed impressively in proportion to every other part of his body and his confidence just made him more attractive. I longed for his name, to see him again.

I couldn't help feeling refreshed seeing everyone, from all friendship groups, getting along. Most of us had been together for a very long time, hardly anyone straying from their own compact, tight-knit friends. Like in most schools, ours had consisted in the normal clicks; the nerds, the Goth like, dark people (these had always freaked me out a little), the plains, the list went on but now everyone was talking. It was like the start of year seven all over again - the categories being irrelevant, everyone being an equal. Andrew had even found himself dancing to a bit of Rihanna and umbrella. It was a bit ironic really, with their not being a cloud in sight, still it was a happy image. There was still no sight of tattoo man, well not yet anyway, so it seemed my only option was to simply join in with the celebrations.

For what seemed like hours, we danced, drank and told ridiculously embarrassing stories from the past two years of college. It was amazing how, for instance, I found myself in deep conversation with Jack about the ice. I was a lover of it; it was my happy place, a place where nothing else mattered. I'd often find myself taking my frustrations out on a rubber puck or through a rather dark but lyrical piece of dance. Ice hockey and Ice Dance were my main sources of relief; it honestly just felt like home. I didn't know Jack was a budding ice fan as well.

For seven years I'd know of him but evidently knew very little about him, automatically branding him as someone I didn't want to befriend. It got me thinking about everyone else in the year, how little we all knew about each other, quick to judge people on their appearance but I guess this was just high school for you. Jack was a speed skater, for the same reasons I enjoyed hammering a puck into a net on an ice hockey rink. Who can blame him with all the stick he used to get? He just never seemed the type. That was just the thing though, everyone jumping to the wrong conclusions. I'd hate to know what people thought about me. We all have this inner confidence because people smiled at you as you walked past, but maybe it was just an act for the horrible things they said behind your back. Secondary school really could be an awful place.

I looked over to Harry and Kieran still trying to sober up Nate. They were useless. The poor guy was lying on the floor pretty much passed out whilst they drew stupid messages on his face. "Jack I'm really sorry but I better go and sort them out" angling towards the boys "It was lovely speaking to you though and good luck with everything. Maybe I'll see you on the ice." I really did mean it; Jack was lovely, a lot chattier than first seemed. Giving him a quick squeeze on the shoulder I got up and walked in the direction of the joke pack, laughing hysterically over the word "knob" embellished now on Nate's forehead. Glancing over towards Jack to give him a 'help me' smile, I saw him. Tattoo man, I mean.

The bar door swung open, two elderly women coming out wearingly looking at each other. A crowd of really drunk eighteen years didn't really look like the company they were used to. He was half hidden, leaning against the inside wall. It was cramped inside the bar but I could tell it was he. His large arm muscles crossed across his front, his detailed tattoos more evident from his bulging muscles. There was that smile again, his white pearls dazzling in the streaming sunlight. It was yet again only another brief glimpse as the door swung back closed again. I looked down at Nate clearly unhappy with his current situation, and then looked back towards the door. Nate, tattoo man, Nate, tattoo man. It was like one of those childhood memories where you used to use the petals on a flower to make a decision. "Guys, I'm just nipping to the toilet, Nate I'll get you some water on the way back" quickly looking down at him apologetically, I then stormed off towards the pub in search for tattoo man.

The pub was dark and crowded from the burst of outside drinkers taking warmth from the temperature drop outside. Poor Nate must be freezing. Normally I'd be straight there dragging him into the warmth but I had my attention on something more important. Tattoo man had obviously moved from just inside the door, obviously avoiding an eighteen-year-old stalker. I had no real plan; following a guy round a pub with the occasional stare was normal right? That's when I saw him at the bar talking to the same barmaid that was flirting with Callum earlier. Of course he was; brunette, skinny and over boisterous girls was clearly more his type than a red haired, faired skinned and typical English girl. Out the corner of my eye I saw Callum, surprisingly standing with Jack. 'You go Jack' I thought, clearly finding a new found confidence. Well at least something good had come from today, just looked like my romance status was staying the same. Callum kept staring at them, visibly sharing the same jealously at me, with his piercing brown eyes. Looking at him I sensed a more protective side, maybe he wasn't all jokes and laughter, maybe he could care like the rest of us.

Attention back to tattoo man, this girl really did have balls, now fully established in her flirting, stroking his arm that laid poised on the bar. I had never been a fan of green-eyed monsters but even I couldn't help myself from painfully staring. How did she do it? She carried such suave, little shame and was undoubtedly one of those girls that didn't stop until she got what she wanted. With drinks ready and payment being paid, tattoo man looked to be making his move; not without the girl handing him a piece of paper. Well it was obvious what was on that. Whipping it into his back pocket he took the drinks and headed into the direction of his two wing men. That's when I saw it; he took out the piece of paper and ripped it in half, throwing its remains into an empty pint glass. "Ha, maybe not so perfect after all" I said to myself feeling most certainly satisfied.

The guys had found themselves a spot in the far corner of the little pub, trying to avoid all the mess and noise us college leavers were making. I couldn't just walk over yet they'd sat themselves in such a position that I couldn't accidentally bump into them. You could say I was a bit rusty at this whole 'asking a guy his name' thing. I really was clueless when it came to men - how to talk to them, how to keep them interested and most stupidly how to get their attention in the first place. Where were my wingmen when I needed them? Remembering Nate lying on the floor in the cold, probably with the forecast rain now falling on him. I can imagine Kieran and Harry found themselves a tree or better still followed me into the pub. To go and help him would have been my normal reaction but then I'd risk losing sight of tattoo man. I'm sure Nate would understand, maybe the water would cure that drunken state anyway.

Frantically looking around, hoping to spot Harry and Kieran, I felt a hand on my shoulder. It wasn't Harry's. Harry had always had the mick taken out of him for his small hands. This was a workingman's hand, one that quite clearly used his hands as part of his job. That ruled Kieran out of the equation too. Trying to use my peripheral vision, I could feel myself freezing yet wanting to turn round. This guy simply just wanted me to move out the way. "Hi" came from behind me. Was he talking to someone in front of me? I glance across the room, no one waving or talking in my direction, all immersed in their own conversation. Either that or they were too drunk to realize. "Kass" I told myself, "You're really starting to look stupid." The grip on my shoulder loosened and then there he was standing right in front of

me. "Nice outfit" he smiled. That smile again. I knew I shouldn't have had that fourth pitcher; my legs had gone weak, my head spinning.
"You've been looking for me," gleaming that smile towards me yet again. Arrogance or what? But still I said nothing. This was my problem, without my three musketeers or Lottie I was a lost cause. You'd have more fun speaking to a brick wall.

"Ok, so clearly not a talker. Maybe a kiss will do the trick instead," he said winking. I didn't even flinch or try to move away. Captivated by the here and now, my legs froze still, utterly in control. His blue eyes were nearly as amazing as his smile, having such depth and happiness. Then there it was, before I knew it he'd kissed me. His warm, soft lips placing a gentle but caring kiss on mine. It wasn't what I'd expected. Pulling away, I kept my eyes on his getting lost in the mystery behind them. Then, giving him the once over, I noticed the words scripted on his inner left forearm. 'For Mum, I love" read the words. A mummy's boy then, maybe he wasn't a heartbreaker like he first appeared. He moved closer yet again, placing another tender kiss, this time on my cheek; before whispering "you smell good." I felt a shiver across my entire body before simply saying "Hi, I'm Kassia, Kass for short." Seriously Kass is that the best you could manage? To make matters worse I found myself holding out a hand. He chuckled, staring straight into my eyes, quite seemingly being oblivious to the bright red circles appearing on my cheeks, then simply shook it back. No name, nothing, just a "would you like a drink? Pimms wasn't it?" Pointing over to his guys, "Go and take a seat, Paul and David will keep an eye on you. Can't have you running away now, can we?" The wink came again, before he turned, walking back to the bar.

"He likes you, you know. " I had just sat down, both men smiling far too wide for their face. "Um, hi I'm Kass," once again the handshake coming out. This was becoming a bit of a signature now, and a rather embarrassing one at that. Here I was, about to be surrounded by three dead-drop gorgeous men and all I could do was say my name and offer a friendly hand. I was an outrage to the female species.

"Ah you managed to keep her here then fellas, I see she offered you the handshake too," winking, then glancing down at my airborne hand. Quickly I put it back in my lap, the other one holding it down into position. I needed to calm down and quick. Taking a sip of my ice cold drink, I tried to steady my nerves.

"So what's your name?" I asked, looking directly at tattoo man.

"She knows more than just a few words guys, she's a keeper," came the response, winking again. I couldn't quite figure this guy out. Was it all just a game to him or was he genuinely interested? Either way something inside me told me to tred carefully with this one - it was clearly my Mother's voice inside my head.

Across the slowly departing bar, I saw Harry and Kieran desperately trying to keep Nate awake. Just seeing them made me instantly relax; Harry's never-ending smile, Kieran's abnormally high laugh and Nate's ever-growing drunken state, letting me know that everything was still normal - that I hadn't gone off in some dream world, imagining what seemed like the last few minutes. With the pub now dispersing at a more rapid rate it had probably been an hour at the least. An hour Kass and all you had achieved was two handshakes, an introduction and one mere question, how pathetic was that? A question I never got a response to…

The boys were failing. Nate clearly needed his bed and how ever much they flicked cold water at him or slapped him round the face that fact was never going to change. Normally I'd be the first to the rescue but I was caught up in my own mess right now; Nate's bedroom furnishings were the last things on my mind. They saw me, waved and then Kieran winked at me, mouthing something that looked like "You go girl." What was it with all this winking? It was like it was a new guy code, one that I needed to get up to speed with and quick. Nevertheless, I couldn't help but feel unease by it all. "So Kassia, Kass for short, do you zone out a lot?" "Huh?" I had no idea what he was on about.

"Well for the past five minutes I've clearly been speaking to myself." The smile was still there so I thankfully hadn't annoyed him too much. I always knew my daydreaming would catch me out one day, I just wished it hadn't been in front of one of the most intriguing guys I had ever spoken to. His friends, Paul and David, were giggling amongst themselves to the right of me. They looked like immature children; had they never seen their friend speak to a girl before? Maybe he was gay or something, knowing my luck that was probably a case. He certainly didn't look it but what was the right way to look? Or maybe all of this was one big joke to them; maybe tattoo man was in on the act too, picking on an innocent and naïve college girl to make fun of. I'd been part of someone's game before. I'd been hurt, used and vowed to myself to never let it happen again. This guy was either seriously troubled or only knew how to use that thing in his trousers, apart from that his chat was somewhat standard, well from what I'd heard anyway – he'd only offered a girl a drink. If only he wasn't so attractive.

Attractive he was. His body was so tensed it was impossible not to imagine what lay underneath his snug-fit white t-shirt. In the dim lighting it was all down to your imagination, something mine had never failed at running wild. Did the tattoos stop at his shoulders, or cover his torso? Were his muscles as pronounced as they looked? And as for down below, was it really as big as it looked? Questions that all needed answers, answers that seemed a light year away. All I could call him was tattoo man, I had no name, and I knew nothing about this man yet none of it seemed relevant. He certainly wasn't a man you'd introduce to your parents and he definitely didn't seem the dating and romance type but I couldn't stop myself from wanting a part of him.

A piece of paper slid towards me on the table. "Maybe you'll speak more by text." He gave me that unforgettable smile, squeezed my arm once more then got up and walked out, before even giving me the chance to find a response. I just stared at the number written down, what was I meant to do with this? I could hardly send a text saying "Hi its Kass." Firstly he really would think I was deluded; secondly I don't think you could send a handshake via mobile. No, if I wanted to see tattoo man again, I needed to get my pulling game back on track. There was only one person I could rely on to help with that...unfortunately he just happened to be the most inebriated person here.

Cream Pie Anyone?

If only decisions were as easy as pulling a few petals out of a flower. The harsh truth was, that romance was hard, men were even harder and the odds of picking a good one were as close to zero as you could possibly get. Love was supposedly a gamble. It was one of those black or red scenarios on a roulette table yet the good ones remained safely in the green zone at the top. It was simply not as easy as 50/50.

Standing outside, letting the cold, countryside airs sweep through my hair I couldn't help but stare at his number. His scruffy handwriting made it hard to work out the digits. It had been a long time since any guy had written his number on an old piece of napkin. Some could say it was quite romantic, others sleezy, saying it had booty call all over it but I just couldn't help but feel numb. The whole experience had been rather odd. The way he just walked up, touched me, kissed me, kissed me again and then just left. There was no introductions, no real goodbyes and I had very little to judge him on. He wasn't a prince charming, that was clear, but the way he held himself, the way his arrogance was outweighed by his insanely good looks, threatened me yet excited me at the same time. For the first time since Adam, I found myself wanting something, wanting Tattoo Man.

The sex would quite clearly be incredible, his muscly arms wrapping you in so tight that you could focus on nothing else but the rhythm of his heartbeat. He seemed the passionate type, the type to know all the right things to say and do. I'd always been a pretty shocking judge of character but there was always time for chance, right? Maybe he wasn't there to use a girl, judge her, and then chuck her; maybe he really was a romantic, a flower and candles kinda guy. Wishful thinking I know, but every girl could dream.

Staring back at the piece of paper, I had now crumbled into a tight ball; I became aware of the noise behind me. Harry, Kieran and a slightly more with it Nate stood looking somewhat concerned.
"Kass what's going on, are you OK?" Harry came to rest a hand on my shoulder, the same one he had, and I couldn't help but flinch.

"Kass talk to us, you look like you've seen a ghost. Did that guy touch you?"

Alternating my look between the paper and the boys I simply replied "No." That's the thing he didn't touch me, yet I still couldn't help feeling used. It was as if I'd wanted him to, expected him to, but the way he had left was nothing but a simple and friendly goodbye – hardly something I could complain about.

I would have normally been flattered, been more interested by his gentleman type of exit but to me something just didn't add up. For starters he looked anything but a gentlemen, and there was something seductive about those kisses that just seemed to scream 'bed;' yet nothing of the kind was even suggested. I debated talking to Nate about my confusion but right now I'd be lucky to get any sensible response. Harry and Kieran were a waste of time, either suggesting 'just go with it' or 'Kass just have some fun,' neither being helpful or sensitive but I suppose that was just them, always thinking with their dick. It was late; a conversation tomorrow would be best, giving me the time to sleep on it. I always did my best thinking in bed.

"Harry seriously I'm all good, he was just being friendly and bought me a drink. No need to get jealous." I nudged him in the side before giving him the most forced smile I could manage – not that he bought it mind. That was the thing with Harry; I couldn't hide anything.

Still, I gave him no chance to question things; "Guy's come on its time for bed. Nate do you want my Dad to take you home, he'll be here in a bit?" Harry lived in the village and Kieran was kipping at his. I took a grunt as a 'yes please' and then did the round of goodbyes to the others. By this time Lottie had disappeared probably chatting to whatever guy would listen to her. She never struggled in conversation like me and certainly wouldn't have frozen like I did. However hard I tried the erotic thoughts of tattoo man wouldn't go. I was kidding myself by trying to convince myself I could forget; for those small moments I was with him, he left so much intrigue it was inevitable I would have to see him again.

———

Dad picked us up five minutes later; "Kassia, you all good? Looks like you've seen a ghost."
"Cheers Dad, you know I'm the pale one. Wonder where I got that from!" replying with that forced smile yet again. I could hardly go into the ins and outs of my encounter; one Dad was never very good at those kinds of conversations and two, there simply was nothing to say. I could hardly go round calling him tattoo man, or saying he kissed me but gave me no information on him, people would just think I made the whole thing up. That was the problem; I was now questioning myself on everything but I knew it was real. Tattoo man was real and the effect he had on my body was something so new and exciting, a text tomorrow couldn't cause any more damage.

Climbing into bed that night was so refreshing. Mum had changed the sheets and plumped my pillows in her usual motherly way that getting undressed didn't seem important. I slept like a baby that night. By that time the drunkenness had worn off so I could hardly blame that but instead I had a solid eight hours of dreaming. I was always one of those people, who could never remember my dreams, being a pretty hard sleeper, but this night was different, they remained so vivid that they almost seemed real. Tattoo man was standing there, in front of me, with that smile – holding a hand that I could never quite reach. It was a frustrating dream yet had the same buzz effect that the man did in real life. If someone was watching I was probably smiling the whole night but it made the decision in the morning that so much easier. I was seeing him again.

Did I text or ring him? Did I leave it a few days or bite the bullet today? All these questions were stopping me from talking to him, that and the fact I had no clue what to say. I'd already rang Nate twice, left him one desperate voicemail and still had had no response. It was only eight in the morning but Nate was one of those people who got up at six regardless of whether it was a Saturday or not. It was his 'thinking' time and apparently it was a nicer time to run; he was an insanely good runner, unlike me - for starters it involved trainers. My bed sounded much more appealing yet this morning; once I had woken up, I struggled staying in it. Nate was either still running or sleeping off those pints and shots he knocked back last night. Still, it left me to toss and turn with my decisions until he replied.

I could hear Mum and Dad, talking downstairs; it was even early for them to be up. Something felt strange about this day already, I couldn't quite describe why but I felt on edge already. Heading downstairs seemed strange also, an unfamiliar black jacket hanging on the banister. It was early on a Saturday morning, who would be calling round at this time? I couldn't make out any extra voice and my sister certainly wasn't old enough to have any guy sleep over. Maybe Dad had bought a new jacket; yet again it looked far too young for a 50-year-old man. Either way sitting on the stairs ear wigging was hardly going to solve the mystery.

"Hey Kass, what you doing sitting on the stairs? Come on love the coffee's on and you can tell me all about your night. Hit it hard did you?" after a brief hug,

I followed my mum into the kitchen. Dad was sitting there on his phone, probably playing a new addition of angry birds, muttering to himself.

"Hey mum, whose jacket is that?" pointing back to the hallway, "Don't tell me Dad's trying to be cool again?"

"Kassia Green, I heard that. Your old man is cool I have you know, but no it's not mine. Far too big for me, needs a guy with big shoulders to fill that one." Dad managed to briefly tear himself away from his phone to give me his friendly wink before going back to the screen.

"Kass you remember my friend, Maggie?" She said this as if I'd been living in a hole for the past eighteen years; Maggie was no one other than her best friend and she was as much a part of this family as I was.

Mum went on to finish, "her son, Senna popped round yesterday to drop me off a cookbook I leant her; he just left his jacket that's all. He'll be round in a bit if you want to go get dressed, he's newly single you know."

Mum always was trying to get me coupled up with her friend's sons. It's not that I wasn't interested, just none of them seemed my type; they just came from 'a good family' apparently.

"Ok Mum, I'll go doll myself. We'll give this one a try." It was our little joke, mum would try and set me up and I'd go along with it.

"That's the spirit Kass, anyway you used to play with him naked in the paddling pool when you were little so you already know each other quite well."

That was just what I wanted to hear; another failure before I'd even met the guy. There was no real point making any effort, so jeans and top would do. Wiping off the remains of last night's makeup, I applied new mascara, filled in the eyebrows and added a bit of pink blusher to make me look less zombie like. There was a quick comb of the hair before tying it up into a messy bun. It was now 9'oclock; there was still nothing from Nate and I'd felt like I'd been up for hours. This was evident from the bags under my eyes. After giving myself the once over in the mirror, I re-dialled Nate's number. There was no doubt about it; I had to speak to him before this guy arrived.

No matter what angle I looked at my reflection from, my original choice of outfit really gave me no justice. The over –baggy top seemed to drench me and my holey jeans now saw more skin than jean. If anything I looked trampy, even if the clothes were of high quality. My messy bun wasn't helping either, and with that I slid open my wardrobe and tried to find something more cheery. Something had to make me look more awake. Flicking through my clothes, I decided on a bright red dress. I'd bought it for a Christmas party last year but in typical Kassia style had forgotten about it and ended up buying another outfit. Putting it on, I instantly regretted my decision. My tan was non-existence and it made me look more zombie like than ever; still it would do. I didn't have any intention of latching onto this guy anyway.

There was still no answer. Nate was never useless, so why pick now? I needed him. I knew he'd had far too much last night. It looked like I was making this decision on my own, but within the next few hours mum's new match up would be downstairs. My Mum could never just hand over the jacket; he'd be invited in for a coffee and slice of cake along with the conversation that would be full of praise for me. I did love her, but at the age of eighteen I could pick my own romances yet I couldn't bring myself to tell her that. I suppose secretly I hoped one of these friend's sons worked out, to make her proud and happy. Little chance of that happening when I looked like a little schoolgirl. Giving myself a long looking over in the mirror, I got interrupted by my phone buzzing on my bed. Nate. I'd wanted to speak to him all morning but, now he was calling, it felt like it was too late, like I'd already made my own decision.

Downstairs Mum was getting a freshly baked cake out the oven. This was the standard routine when a perspective fella was coming round; I'd make the small talk, smile in all the right places and he'd leave never to be spoken to again. Mum spotted me on the stairs, "What is it with you and stairs today Kass? You look amazing by the way, new dress?" I looked down at my newly, still labeled red River Island dress, giving it the smooth down. It did look nice, not my usual attire but quite sexy to say the least. "Oh you know it's just something I chucked on" I said, "Where's dad hiding?" Mum was frantically busying herself around; now moving on to the duster. Seriously who was this man, he was only a son of Maggie's; hardly someone you needed to roll a red carpet down for. I knew today seemed strange the minute I woke up, and the more the minutes ticked, the more I felt apprehensive.

My phoned buzzed again in my hand. Nate again. I had to answer; I'd probably worried him senseless with my frantic calling this morning. "Hey you how's the head?"

"Kass what's going on? You acted strange last night then all these calls this morning. It's about that guy isn't it? I knew there was something more to it."

Obviously his head wasn't too bad then. Nate knew I was trying to ignore the problem I was having.

"Nate I'm all good, I was just getting myself into a panic as to whether to call him or not. Like I said, nothing happened. Anyway I better go, Mum's got people coming round for morning coffee." I had to get rid of him before he insisted on answers. Nate was known for his integrations. He was quite but when it came to me he was protective.

"Ok Kass, I'll call you later as long as you are sure you're ok?" Nate sounded worried but if I paid attention to it I'd be on the phone for the next two hours, having to spill all the details. "Love you Nate" and with that I put the phone down.

I knew I should have chattered to him longer, after the pestering this morning, but I'd already decided to text tattoo man – I would just get this coffee morning out the way first. At least that would give me a few hours to decide on what to write. It was now 10:30 and Mum and Dad were sitting at the breakfast bar talking about holidays. They normally did this whenever they had to fill the time; as for me I gave myself one more look over before joining them in the kitchen.

"How was Nate love?" Mum loved Nate, just like she loved all the boys; it took a bit longer for her to warm to Lottie but I think we were getting there. It wasn't that she didn't like her; Lottie just has a certain humour that 60's babies didn't seem to get.

"You know Nate, Mum. He worries too much, think that heads bothering him though." I could hardly let on that there was a mystery man when she had her own arriving anytime soon.

"Mum I thought he was just popping round to pick a jacket up, not a five star banquet?" I said after she was popping other savoury snacks onto plates.

"Oh darling, didn't your Dad mention it? We're turning it into a lunch, Maggie and Bob are coming round too along with their nephew Adam who's around for the weekend." I flinched at the name. Ever since my disastrous on, off heartbreak with Adam I'd completely gone off the name, and chefs for that matter. For what sounded like a cosy get together to my Mum, sounded much more like a full on quest to find me a man. I'm glad I had changed out of my scruffs.

My mind was preoccupied when the doorbell rang. I was sitting outside enjoying the mid morning sun, trying not to look interested in the slightest. Mum, unfortunately was having none of it, "Kass get the door for me whilst I get a new pot of coffee on, and darling try smiling. The hangover can't be too bad." She had no idea. It wasn't that I'd drank a lot, and it certainly wasn't one of those typical drink related ones; it was simply guy related.

Maggie and Bob gave me a beaming smile before engulfing me into their typical bear hug. These were Mum's closet friends, the friends that had seen us all at our worst, shared all our (mainly mine) ups and downs. They brought such a refreshing atmosphere; that was until I looked up to see them – the last two men I ever expected to see. To the left stood Adam, the man who broke my heart on more than one occasion, and to the right Tattoo Man, the mystery man who was more than likely a heartbreaker too. They were standing on my front porch looking at me like we'd never even met. Rewind a year, and Adam would have been greeted with a fist but now all I could feel was numb. I was dumbfounded and my face obviously showed it; "Hi Kass" he said nervously.

For the past 12 months I had gone through this scenario, what I'd say to him, how I'd greet him. I'd promised myself I'd remain dignified, calm, and the last thing I'd do was let him see the damage he had done, but now was a completely different situation. It was those words, I know only simple, but he had no right. "Don't you dare call me that" and with that I turned and ran straight upstairs, tears, uncontrollably, running down my face. The clouds had opened and for the first time since his last goodbye, I cried. Adam was my first love, yet the one that made me so scared to love. He'd broken my heart more times than I could remember, each time turning it on me. I 'deserved better' apparently, each time him disappearing only for me to take him back.

I was seventeen when I met him; I'd fallen in love instantly and was too naïve to realise disaster was just around the corner. He was 4 years my senior, and already an established chef. He wooed me with his gentleman charm, sparkling blue eyes and simple outlook on life. I honestly thought I'd found my prince charming. That was probably the problem; he could do nothing wrong. I'd believed him when he said it was my fault, I'd believed him when he said he loved me but the one thing I couldn't believe was that I deserved better. I wanted him and I thought he wanted me. He did for so long, and then just when I thought we were good he'd drop me for someone more fun just to come running back. The routine went on like this for over a year before he disappeared for good, breaking not only my heart but my trust in mankind too.

A knock came from the door "Kass, I'm so sorry I didn't know it was your Adam." Mum had been my rock throughout the entire Adam saga; she was my shoulder to cry on. He wasn't my Adam anymore; he was a stranger. A stranger standing in my house; a stranger that's related to Tattoo Man, how could I face him now? A beautiful man was standing downstairs probably dumbstruck at what just happened. That's unless Adam had told him everything, which was highly unlikely. Mum came walking in, clearly unsure on what to say. I could see it now - my mascara undoubtedly streaking down my face, eyes puffy and freckles appearing through my patchy foundation. I was definitely not prepared for who followed her. Tattoo Man stood leaning against the doorpost, "Hi Kass" and with that my mum got up and left us staring silently at each other.

Some warning would have been nice; the sight could hardly be attractive. He came and sat next to me and we sat in silence for what seemed like ages. We didn't speak, we didn't touch; we just looked at the floor. Whether he just didn't know what to say, I didn't know, but his presence was felt either way. The tension was intense. Here sat next to me one of the sexiest, most mysterious guys I'd ever met yet he was the cousin of a guy I couldn't bare seeing let alone having any further connection to.

He eventually put his hand on my shoulder, just like he had in The Baggers, and somehow the tension dropped; it felt surprisingly normal. "Kass, are you ok? You don't have to tell me anything, Adam's an idiot, always has been, always will be but from your reaction I'm guessing you were another one of his girlfriend victims?" I nodded my head, it was all I could manage and counting the dust particles on the floor seemed to stop the tears. He was no longer Tattoo Man; he was Senna - a sweet gentleman who seemed to actually care. The way he askcd was so soft and calming, I couldn't help but feel relaxed.

We sat there for a while longer, Senna now holding me, his big muscles engulfing me so tight that it was hard not to feel safe. The anger disappeared and with the occasional gentle forehead kiss I changed from feeling fired up to a strong individual. Adam had done enough damage without destroying my life even more. "I'm sorry," I whimpered, looking up at him. His eyes were bigger than what I remembered, providing so much more enigma. There were no bright red chinos, no tight white t-shirt but there sat a man in ripped baggy jeans and a checked long sleeve shirt. He still looked as gorgeous as ever even without his tattoos on show. There was so much I wanted to know about this man, but right now little conversation was perfect. "You have nothing to be sorry for" he said stroking my hair, "do you want me to bring you some food up, your Mum's made a lovely spread? Or do you fancy coming down with me? Maybe she has some cream pie for that cousin of mine," and with that he stood up and held out his hand. It almost seemed our inside joke; I stood up shook his hand then got pulled into another hug before he whispered "you are funny Kass, beautiful but funny."

I'd known this guy a matter of 24 hours and we already had our own 'thing.' Everything seemed so easy with Senna and for the first time since Adam I felt I could believe whatever he said. All any girl wanted was to feel safe and loved, something Adam failed at. I was now staring at myself in the mirror. Senna was downstairs talking to mum whilst I tidied myself up. After wiping off the panda eyes and applying new mascara, I looked semi reasonable again; time to face the music, time to face Adam.

I found them in the kitchen. Mum and Dad were engrossed in conversation with Senna, Maggie and Bob were cooing over our new pug puppy and Adam was nowhere to be seen. I felt relieved but found myself asking anyway "where is he?" It came across so bluntly I even shocked myself but even the thought of seeing him made my blood boil. Following Mum and Dad's glance down the bottom of the garden, I saw him staring at the wall. "How's my baby girl?" Dad's calming voice was just what I needed. Even though my sister was six years younger I always had been his baby. Seeing him though, surprised me. I felt nothing but pity; still, ignoring him and putting on a happy act wouldn't hurt.

Mum always did know how to put on a good spread and surprisingly the rest of the afternoon ran quite smoothly. Adam stayed where he belonged, with the rest of us playing and patting with Belle. She was the happy vibe we all needed. I'd always imagined having a dog, similar to the ones you saw in the movies - Hollywood stars carrying them in their Prada's. Even though it wasn't Hollywood and I didn't own a Prada, Belle was the perfect addition nonetheless. She loved Senna and I couldn't help but smile watching her lick his face. There was nothing strange about this man, nothing to be worried about and so for once I just let things be.

It was the evening before we knew it, drinks flowing and Adam still sitting quietly at the bottom of the garden. I had no desire to invite him up. Mum brought out her signature victoria sponge, along with mudcake for the fussy 'no cream' eaters like me. I saw him wink and instantly knew what he was on about. Senna's connection and mine was indescribable yet we seemed very much on the same page. "Cream cake will do," flashing that smile of his. The rest of the table was totally oblivious but I couldn't help but laugh and with that he cut and extra slice and stormed off down the garden. I didn't believe he'd actually do it. It was like watching it in slow motion, gasps and 'Senna's' being shouted around me.

Adam's face was covered in cream; his perfect looks now being dented by the white mixture that disguised it. It was funny; no one could deny that. Mum and Maggie looked utterly shocked, Dad and Bob being Senna's own support party. It was safe to say I wasn't on my own when it came to not liking Adam. If only there was a camera to capture the moment. Senna came strolling back to be greeted with high fives by the fathers. I just sat there in disbelief that someone would actually do that for me. He hardly knew me yet had creamed his own cousin over a past he didn't know the facts about. Maybe he just hated his cousin as much as I did, or maybe, just maybe, he liked me enough to risk the wrath from his mother.

The atmosphere for the next few hours was rather upbeat - the wine and beer fully flowing. Adam had remained on his own, surprising everyone that he stayed instead of going home. He hadn't even wiped the cream off, just merely left it, smearing it out of his eyes. When it reached midnight the Jackson's left. The usual round of hugs took place. There really was nothing not to like about Maggie and Bob; they'd been part of my life since the start and had been my second Mum and Dad for my junior years. They knew things I was too scared to tell my own parents, like when I first started my period, taking it upon themselves to tell them in a way they'd understand. I hadn't seen them for ages, and hadn't apparently seen Senna since I was 4. From what I understood, he was sent off to private school as a troubled kid but now he stood in front of me looking nothing but perfect. Before leaving he whispered a simple 'bye Kass," held out his hand, in which I shook without hesitation, and walked down the path with his parents and a sulky looking, creamed faced Adam. Tattoo Man paused when he reached the end, "Kass I'll text you," and with that he climbed into the back of the car. With the sight, I couldn't help but inwardly chuckle before silently hugging both my parents and slipping off to bed.

An Erotic Dream

For the second night running I slept like a baby. I always did loving sleeping but lately I'd struggled with the temperamental English weather, that and the pressures that now stood in front of me. I was a college leaver, off to university something that no one in my family had ever done. Then there was the pressure of actually finishing the degree, settling down and starting a family. My family had always been traditionalists seeing this as the right way of doing things but as I'd always struggled on finding and keeping love the middle part was something I thought would never happen.

That night I couldn't help but dream of Senna. There was something to his name that made the whole situation seem romantic but the dream was far from that, instead his nickname 'tattoo man' seemed much more appropriate. It was dark and only the light came from streetlight outside my bedroom window. Tattoo Man was stood with his back to me, appearing nothing but a silhouette. The room was silent with nothing to be heard but our extreme breathing. I woke up immediately, my breathing still heavy. The dream was so vivid I remembered all the details - his touch, his kiss and his smell, all making me want it for real.

I'd never really thought of a guy in this way before. I was known as a sweet and innocent girl, a label I happily took to. Guys were to be gentlemen and romantic otherwise I wouldn't even look at them. This dream proved all that wrong. I, like most eighteen-year-old girls and boys, had fascinations and clearly desired him. Tattoo Man seemed a distraction even when he wasn't physically around; he drifted in and out of my thoughts every other minute and took over my sleep too. I couldn't help but hope and wonder whether he felt anything of the sort or whether it was all one-way traffic.

My thoughts came back to his actions of the previous evening, where he'd stuck up for me without evening knowing the details. Without meaning to, my lips turned into a smile and before I could stop myself I started crying. Grabbing my teddy next to me and hugging it so tight as to stop the whimpering sounds, I cried – long and hard until I had no more tears to cry. Cooky had been my teddy since I was ten and even at the age of eighteen he gave me all the comfort I needed. Truth is I had no explanation as to where the tears came from. I certainly didn't feel upset; Tattoo Man was all I'd ever wanted and more, but for some reason I felt ashamed. Maybe it was down to wanting a man that was clearly too good for me, maybe it was down to not having the confidence to act on my feelings or maybe it was down to the shear fact of feeling disgusted at the dream I'd just had.

Rewinding back, the dream was far more erotic than first described. I'd gone to bed like normal, wearing my red Hollister pyjamas. They were my favourite; with their cute little shorts that just molded the bum perfectly so not to ride up - so cute, yes, sexy definitely not. I slowly fell asleep with my headphones in, listening to some calming whale music; it had been the only thing that had got me to sleep since the ordeals of Adam. I'd never been one for remembering dreams but this one seemed to have purpose, seemed to have meaning. I couldn't quite pinpoint the exact moment Senna had come into my thoughts but it now seemed impossible to get him out of them.

Senna had come in my room wearing nothing but his boxer shorts. He could have been naked for all I knew. In fact, it could have been anyone as I could only just make out a silhouette through my tired eyes. It wasn't until he stepped closer to where I was sleeping that I recognised his scent. That warm, musky one I remembered from our earlier embrace. I'd reached out my hand managing to touch his bare skin before he gently removed it. "Senna" I'd whispered. I was surprised he'd heard me; my mouth was so dry and my heart pounded so hard that even I thought it was about to give up at any time. "Not yet Kassia" his voice sounded so gentle yet in control. He knew he had me, had my attention.

He came and sat on the edge of my bed without saying another word. I sat up, automatically pulling my pyjama top trying to keep my dignity in tack. The darkness that surrounded us wouldn't have shown anything but I somehow felt like I was going to mentally need all the help I could get. Senna sat a breath away, and all I could do is want him.

The dream carried on in the way anyone would expect, but for me it was a completely new experience. We sat there for what seemed like forever until he placed a gentle kiss on my forehead. That was it, it was at that moment I knew I was falling for him. Even though it was only a dream, the feelings were real. There was something about that night that seemed to change me.

I knew it was a terrible idea, letting him into my head, but somehow I couldn't stop it. He seemed so perfect it was hard not to fall for his irresistible charm. His deep brown eyes were now at the forefront of my mind but the real question remained in what he was hiding behind them. I'd learnt from his cousin that men with a clearly cute but cocky outer persona were the ones that seemed to break your heart the most. That was the problem; my heart probably hadn't even fixed after it's first ordeal and yet there I lay debating about whether I should take the risk with another obvious heartbreaker.

I don't know where they came from but tears started rolling down my face again. I'd only known of this guy for 48 hours and still he'd managed to make me cry twice. He was the perfect gentleman, the kind of man every 18 year-old would want but my heart was scared and that was one hurdle I was struggling to jump over. It wasn't Senna's fault; Mum would say I couldn't even blame myself but no matter whose fault it was, it just wasn't fair.

The early morning sun starting streaming through my curtains, that's when I realized the chance of getting anymore sleep was unrealistic. I quickly checked my phone to see if I'd received the text; my heart sank when I saw the screen blank, yet again he was probably still asleep. Slipping into my new workout gear I decided on a brisk morning run in hope of trying to clear my head and get Senna out of it before anymore damage could be done. The house was quiet with everyone else enjoying a Sunday morning lie in, that's when I looked at the clock to realize it had only just gone six. Part of me was surprised it was even that late. I had one more look around the living room, which was messed with the last remaining leftovers of last night then plugged myself in. Ironically the first song was 'Best Mistakes', one of my sister's favourite Ariana Grande songs. It seemed almost apt but after a quick listen to the chorus I touched the next button to find something more appropriate.

The crisp air was a relief. After my dream last night I'd woken up with a rather unattractive sweat, luckily the streets were as quiet as my house with only the occasional car going past. Normally my jogs were simply that; a jog, but this morning my legs were moving faster, my frustrations clearly taking over. Song after song, my fear and anger seemed to be going and for the first time in the past two days I felt back in control. Senna was just a guy, whose mum was a friend of mine and Adam was simply a mistake. I didn't need a guy, not one that would only cause more heartbreak.

An hour later I was back at home hardly being able to stand yet feeling refreshed and still my inbox was empty. Maybe his phone had broken or maybe he didn't have my number. I'd never actually given it him but I knew Maggie had it. Maybe she was refusing to give it him. All the possible scenarios ran wild round my head but I tried to remain positive. He really was probably still asleep, or at work. He was really was probably still asleep, or at work. What did he even do? I made myself a mental note to ask him when he text me; which he was totally going to do.

Everyone was clearly still asleep; with there being no evidence of the usual fresh coffee aroma that normally filled the kitchen at weekends. Before jumping into the shower, I got to work with clearing the empty wine bottles and plating up the remaining nibbles. The room was starting to look back to how it should when I felt someone watching me. "Darling are you ok? You're cleaning."

"Hi to you too mum." There was that worried look across her face, probably more down to that fact I was awake rather than I doing housework. The last thing I wanted was to be quizzed after I'd just spent the last hour detoxing my emotions. That was the thing, I knew my mother too well just like she did me. She knew when I was distracted and her radar was even more on the ball when it involved a guy. I needed to get out of the room, at least until other people were around. "Mum I'm fine, seriously, sit down I'll put the coffee machine on then jump in the shower." Hopefully that would pause the conversation…at least for now.

Swallow

I managed to avoid 'that' conversation with my mum for the rest of the day making sure either my sister or dad was present. My phone was glued to my side, with me frequently checking and hoping for a text. It never came, but still I remained stupidly optimistic. That night I dreamed of everything but Senna, with the ordeals of the past two days nothing but a distant memory. Truth is I saw no real reason why I'd bump into Adam or Senna again; I only had a few months to get through until I started my new adventures in Manchester. I told myself Manchester would house better males and even though I knew it was optimistic it was the only thing stopping me from messaging Senna.

I woke up the following day to the hustle of my mum hurrying my sister out the door to school. My sister and I were nothing alike, she was so laid back doing everything at the slowest pace going whereas I liked structure. It made me smile, now don't get me wrong I love my sister to pieces but sometimes she really did make hard work of everything. The door slammed behind her before mum walked back upstairs to carry on her morning routine of watching Jeremy Kyle. I laid there and plugged myself in waiting for the get up knock I had been used to ever since I finished the everyday school timetable. Whilst the songs played I contemplated messaging Tattoo Man first. There was no rule to say girls couldn't, we just often didn't have the confidence to do so; afraid of being ignored or even worse, told to go away. I picked up my phone from next to me and opened a new message; I started typing,

"Hi Senna, it's Kassia Green."

Ok, so maybe that was a little too formal, I thought as I started deleting it. I'm sure he only knew one Kass, well I hoped he did anyway. In the end I opted for short and sweet message of,

"Hi Senna, it's Kass. How are you? Thanks for last night, I had fun. Xxx"

Was three kisses too full on? Before sending I deleted one and went with two, nicely in the middle. There, now I would get a reply.

An hour later the knock came. Mum had promised me to lunch today at The Swallow, and even though it seemed like there was a hidden agenda to get me to talk I couldn't refuse. The Swallow was a small countryside pub, the kind with the low ceilings and one that always seemed to have atmosphere no matter what time of day it was. It attracted customers from all over the vale and seemed a must visit place for travellers. Not only that but they served the most delicious steak fajitas.

I've always had a weird obsession over steak. Harrison always said my love for meat was almost too manly. That's the thing; my Mum knew it was my weakness and she planned to exploit it. I stood looking at my reflection in the mirror. My hair needed a wash, my eyes looked tired and my cheeks, no matter how much I tried to cover them, looked too red and rosey for my liking. I needed some excitement in my life; I looked dull and definitely not like someone that had just finished my college years but first came this lunch and that dreaded conversation. Throwing on some black skinny jeans and a cute, but non-flattering top I was ready, well as ready as a daughter could be to be integrated by her mother.

I knew my mother cared; she'd been there through every up and down I ever went through with Adam. There was that name again, there was no avoiding it. He taught me so much but gave so much heartache at the same time. My mum was my rock. We shared every tear, every box of chocolates and watched every rom-com we had in the house but now she clearly wanted to talk and no matter how hard I tried to avoid it I knew it needed to happen. My Mum could make me feel better even when she didn't try to.

"Kassia, darling, are you ready?" Mum was calling from downstairs. Looking at the clock, I hadn't realized two hours had gone by. One more glance in the mirror and well, I didn't have much to show for it but I didn't plan on seeing anyone else anyway. Mum had seen me at my worse and I certainly didn't look that bad. I quickly checked my phone to see if he'd read my message. My heart missed a beat as I saw the read sign under the blue bubble, yet there was no reply. I was momentarily sad before deciding he was probably just busy and that he would reply later. Last night was too nice for him not too. I slid my iPhone into my back pocket before finding some shoes to wear. Zipping up my Chelsea boots and after applying a little gloss to my lips I was ready for some steak.

It was weird; I hadn't noticed how beautiful the Vale was before. I'd always driven down its country lanes in the dark often sat in the back of my Dad's car, but now I was able to see it for its true beauty. The fields were large and quiet, with only the odd dog walker spoiling the view. The sun was peering over the castle ahead. Mum was muttering, probably singing along to the radio under her breathe. The sound of Adele's "Hello" filled the car; the mellow tones instantly vanishing all thoughts of the night before. It wasn't that I wanted to forget Tattoo Man but just put him on pause for a day or two, just until I was ready to face the consequences of falling for someone again.

Pulling into The Swallow's grounds was like arriving in a fairytale. It's grounds were so expansive that people were able to enjoy peace and quiet whilst being amongst so many people. It was hard not to feel calm and at ease. Birds were chirping in the long row of trees that surrounded the park with the main building hidden just behind them. Mum and I walked along the path in silence, taking in the summer air; that's when I saw it. The staff's car park was at the side of the restored mansion. With it being a Monday lunch time only a few cars were parked up. It wasn't hard to spot, the same car was only parked outside mine a few days ago. With its superior matte finish and its sparkling alloys, the BMW stood out from all the others. Mum seemed to spot it too, "Oh Kass, Maggie and Bob might be here." She tried to sound enthusiastic but even she wasn't convinced. Why would they park in the staff car park anyway?

Part of me wanted to run back to car, part of me told me I was being stupid and it was just some crazy coincidence but then there was that small part of me that was intrigued; hoping to see Tattoo Man again. Even my Mum's slight squeeze on my shoulder couldn't have prepared me for what was coming.

It was hard to explain. He hadn't done anything; maybe he hadn't deliberately meant to hurt me. He'd only chosen not to reply to my message and then smile at me. The smile was probably his way of being friendly, or maybe it was his way of apologising for not responding; either way it reminded me of the way Adam had acted before one of his many disappearing acts. Tattoo man was something else though, something that you'd only dream of, something you only wanted to dream of. I was well aware I had drifted off into another daydream. These were coming more and more regular these days; ever since Tattoo Man had entered my life...

"Kass are you ready" Mum was looking at me with those worried eyes of hers. I looked down at my half-eaten steak, knife and fork still clenched in my hands. Mum would know something was up; I never left a steak dinner. Truth is, ever since I saw him walk out of those kitchen doors, my head and stomach seemed to leave the room. I couldn't seem to come up with any conversation and my appetite was made up of small nibbles of chips and lettuce. It was time to leave.

"Sorry Mum, can we go?" I tried to give her a reassuring look but I obviously failed. My Mum was someone else, she knew my thought process better than I did myself, but even she knew now was not the time. Standing up, she collected the coats, paid the bill then came back to collect me; her little girl, her little girl with the same guy problems. I couldn't help but feel a let-down. Recently, well ever since Adam, it was hard to find a real smile, to really feel happy. Don't get me wrong I faked it well but only to those didn't know me. All my Mum wanted was a happy girl, one that was settled, one that she could marry off and someone she could be proud of. At this moment in time, I let her down in all departments.

The Swallow's grounds had always been photogenic. The unusual summer's sun was reflecting off the long-featured pond, not only creating an overall glow over the extensive grounds but bringing an atmosphere that instantly relaxed you. I wanted to run as far away as possible yet wanting to soak in every emotion the garden had to offer. An elderly couple were walking on the other side of the pond hand in hand. You couldn't help but smile. Now that was true love. It brought me back to something my Nan had once said "Kassia, when I was your age if something was broken, we had to fix it, we didn't know how to run away." If only all relationships had that moral now.

For a moment, I'd forgotten the events of earlier. My mum was standing a few yards in front of me also staring at this couple. We were so alike when it came to romance. It was a must; there was nothing it couldn't fix. That feeling of being loved, a kiss and a cuddle and a good old spoon at night. It was the definition of a bad day cure. This couple probably had had their differences like every other pair out there but something seemed rawer, more real. The elderly gentleman clearly adored this woman, which I could only assume to be his wife. It was the kind of love that I imagined my parents to have. That everlasting kind, the kind that was only seen in fairy tales.

"Kass are you coming?" Mum was now staring at me, taking her attention away from the couple. One last glance over the pond then I joined my Mum at the entrance to the car park. She grabbed my arm and rustled her nose in my hair. It was her favourite past time, something that apparently used to make me laugh as a baby. It was a shame it didn't have the same effect. Now it just made me well up. There was something about the country air today that was making me an emotional wreck. I felt useless, worthless and more depressingly, unwanted. Tattoo Man had only just come into my life and I already wanted him gone.

The short car journey home was silent. My mum stayed quiet, probably unsure of what to say and I, well I just fell into my happy place. I daydreamed about everything but Tattoo Man; seeing myself ruining through the open fields that surrounded us. I almost imagined it like a scene from Dirty Dancing, where Babe was throwing herself into jumps. It was then I found myself feeling alone again. It surrounded you everywhere. Love; it was only a small four letter word, scoring you no more than six points on a scrabble board, yet it carried such power. If it wasn't a personal battle, the one between myself and love, I'd encourage people to find it, embrace it and never let it go.

"Darling are you going to answer that?" It was then I realised we were home, sitting stationary on the driveway. My phone was ringing in my bag, that usual iPhone ringtone filling the car with invited sound. "Sorry Mum I was miles away" I said getting my phone and seeing the caller ID. It was Nate, a lovely distraction but one that would have to wait until later. Setting the phone to silent I quickly stuffed it back in my bag and reached for the door handle. "Kass, wait, I'm worried about you" "Mum I'm…"
"Don't even try and tell me you're fine Kass. Not only did you leave half a steak, but the way you acted back then was out of character. You've always been so friendly with everyone."

I wanted to tell her she was wrong, that the way I acted was completely normal and not the least bit psychotic but I couldn't. Like usual she was right, I was always known for giving everyone the benefit of the doubt, for being everyone's friend but today I couldn't find it in me. I'd flipped at the sight of him…again.

I hadn't seen Adam since the last time he broke my heart. It wasn't luck. I'd deliberately been avoiding all contact with anyone called Adam, let alone my Adam, and now I'd seen him twice in the space of two days. This time seemed worse than the first. I shivered at the reminder. I was sitting back in the restaurant, enjoying a nice lunch with my Mum, that's when I saw them; Tattoo Man and my Adam standing in the entrance to the kitchen, laughing away; until they saw me. Both stood in chef whites, their laughing abruptly ending. Their shock was evident and was a mirror image of my own. Tattoo man directed a smile my way, holding something that looked pretty much like his phone; Adam on the other hand just stared, probably unsure on what my reaction would be. My lack of self-confidence had sent my brain into overdrive, automatically assuming they were talking and laughing about me.

My reaction was probably unjustified; in fact, I knew it was. Sitting here now I was ashamed. I'd acted with no dignity and not only embarrassed myself but also made all the eaters gasp and stare, not forgetting the appalled look on my mother's face. I wouldn't be forgetting that one in a while, the look of disapproval, the look of shear embarrassment. The Shallow's had gone from my favourite place in the Vale to the worst in the space of a few hours.

Drops of rain had started appearing on the windscreen. That's when I realised the reality of the situation; I wasn't going to be allowed to move, not until I'd explained my actions. Why had I burst over to the pair of them? Why had I wasted a glass of wine, expensive wine should I add, by throwing it over their chef whites? And more importantly why had I let them bother me? If only I knew the answers. It was only less than twenty-four hours ago that I was having saucy yet unrealistic dreams about one of the men. Mum was now staring at me clearly waiting for an answer, some sign that her daughter was still sane. "Mum I'm sorry, I don't know what else I can say." Truth is I knew what she wanted to hear but I could hardly admit it was all down to a non-replied to message. Somehow, I couldn't find the reassurance she longed for so I just looked long and hard at my lap hoping that that was the end of that. I wanted to tell her it wasn't the same as before but part of me felt it was. Adam had screwed my head and emotions up from day one, making me act out of character, to the disarray of my family.

Something was telling me it was the same. I'd got on another emotional roundabout that would take ages to get off. Nobody would understand; understand how one guy could have such an effect on one eighteen-year-old girl. Once again I found myself hating the opposite sex but this time it was without even properly getting involved with them. The problem had to be me, then again that could just be my insecurities talking. Tattoo Man looked at me in a way that cut into my heart, making a scar that seemed almost impossible to fix. It was one of those things that us girls had to put up with; heartbreak. This time I couldn't even blame him, it was Adam that hit a nerve, it was Adam that made me flip but it was Senna that paid the price. Any chance of further encounters was demolished in just a few actions.

I wanted to cry. The weather had changed with the progression of the day, with the rain now pounding down. I looked at my Mum before getting out the car, standing there, letting the rain batter my pale white skin. It was refreshing. Hoping to wash away all the stress and anxiety that propelled throughout my body, I stood there for what seem like hours. I remained completely oblivious to the glares from neighbours. Even in the privacy of an enclosed cul-de-sac I couldn't be alone. My problems and emotions were real and that was something I would just have to face.

The rain was starting to hurt now; red welts appearing all over my forearms. Mum came from behind me, armed with an umbrella, "Feel better?" she asked. I gathered she knew the answer but I gave a brief nod of the head before we hurried through the gate and under cover. I did feel better to a certain extent or at least I'd realised I couldn't go through another Adam saga all over again. Tattoo Man was nice while it lasted, I'd just have to stay clear of Maggie and Bob for a while.

The rain helped in some ways but washing away all embarrassment was a bit far stretched.

I was a drowned rat. Looking at my reflection in the mirror, I couldn't help but feel ashamed. My pale skin, my now black eyes and my dripping hair were all signs of someone that needed a new direction in life. I couldn't help but weep. Adam was still finding ways of destroying my life but now he was dragging possible new candidates into his twisted world. I knew this wasn't theoretically true and that they were in fact related but it seemed easier blaming him than it did facing my own wrong doings. I kept replaying the two minutes that changed everything in my head. All Senna had done was smile and before my outburst it was probably a sign of him being happy to see me. I'd simply punished him for being related to an ex.

Stripping down to my bra and knickers I couldn't help but smile. I'd obviously woken up feeling even the smallest bit of happiness as I was wearing one of my favourite Victoria Secret's lingerie sets. I'd always lived to the motto that matching underwear meant a positive day; if only today could have been. Removing the remainder of my sodden clothing I stepped into a more favourable downfall. The warm water was a relief yet plummeted a sensational burn over my body. It took all my strength to not keep going over the events of earlier. Instead I tried focusing on ways of moving on. It was only a few months then I'd be moving to university, far away from all the embarrassment of the previous few days, far away from Senna and most importantly several miles away from Adam. I planned to enjoy the next months with people that brought the best out in me, starting with replying to Nate. I quickly washed my hair, shaved my legs, although a pointless exercise as no guy was going near them anytime soon, and jumped out of the shower.

Mum was on the phone downstairs so I took the time to talk to Nate in private. He'd be an invited distraction, as he always was. Maybe a get to together with the boys was a good starting point to moving on. Dialling Nate's number, I heard Mum filling someone in "I'm worried, it's really not like her." Based on her tone it was either to Maggie or my father. I knew she'd talk to them, I just hoped she wouldn't. Either way I wasn't going to let it bother me. If it was to my father, then a conversation would more than likely be taking place when he got in from work. If it was Maggie, then she'd probably invite herself around to check in on me. I'd need to find my convincing "I'm fine" a-game and quick.

"Hey stranger" Nate's voice instantly soothed you. I could imagine his cheeky grin at the end of the line. "You saw me three days ago Nate"
"Kass that's a long time to go without speaking to your number one girl." Nate loved to remind me I was his, much to Harrison's dismay. That was the thing about having three best mates that were all guys. They all loved the attention and they all loved the competition. Harrison was more than a best mate, we had an extra connection but he was one of those guys that could disappear off the radar at the most inconvenient moments. Nate on the other hand was always there.

"Sorry Nate, you know how it is."

"With you Kass, that normally means a guy."

I could tell where he was going with this. It normally began with an 'A' and ended with 'M'. I wanted to jump in before he could ask but he was far too quick to carry on.

"It better not be anyone like that Adam guy otherwise I can't tell you what I'd do." There was humour in his voice but I could tell he was serious. Thing is, Nate wouldn't win in any fight. He had muscle but he had a heart of gold; I guess the thought was there though. That was the thing with Nate, he knew he'd lose, probably end up with scratches over his prize possession but for the people he loved he'd do anything.

"Nate everything's fine, I've just been busy that's all." Even I was impressed by the convincing tone to my voice but if anyone could read through it was Nate. There was a slight pause on the other end of the line but then back came the reply of "Ok Kass, well you know where I am if you need me." He knew something was up but clearly went with the safer option of not pushing the truth out of me. The topic of conversation was soon changed, mainly planning our next few months together. It was hard to think that our group was splitting up in all different directions of the country. There were to be no more quick visits, spontaneous trips out or most tragically, no more memories built on a daily basis. It broke my heart but we intended to make the most of the summer, starting with the weekend and a much loved shopping trip.

The boys were just like me. They loved to shop and would often come back with more bags than me. I planned to use it as a distraction, hoping that Harrison would bring his top humour game and that I'd come home with laughter stitches. Nate and mine's conversation went on for what seemed like hours. At least phone conversations were something that even separate universities couldn't stop. By the time we'd said our goodbyes my hair was semi-dry and my shoulders were somewhat cold. Quickly exchanging the towel for my white fleecy dressing gown, I gave my hair one last shake with the towel before heading downstairs to face whatever music was waiting for me. My phone buzzed half way on my descent; the front screen of my iPhone flashed Harrison's name, making me instantly smile. I placed the phone back in my pocket; the message could wait until later.

The TV was on. Mum was catching up on one of her daily soaps, probably waiting for Malia to get in from school. I paused before entering, wondering whether it was a good idea to enter or whether darting back upstairs was the safer option. The latter certainly seemed more enticing but Mum was too quick; "Kass." I walked in, trying not to catch eye contact, and was surprisingly welcomed with a hug. It wasn't just any kind of hug, it was the kind that said "it's ok," and instantly it was. I knew I wasn't going to be quizzed and I knew she would try her best to understand. It was all the reassurance I needed.

The next few hours seemed like any other day. Granted it was strange not being a college girl coming in with my sister but it felt normal nonetheless. Malia came in from school, dropped her school bag near the front day and joined us on the sofa. I looked at her almost longing to be her age again; an innocent thirteen year old who had no idea of the issues that lay ahead of her. At that age every romance is a fairytale; the kind you watch on the big screens or the ones you read about in books. She had no idea and I wasn't about to be the one to ruin that for her. "How was school Mal?" My sister was one of those girls that had already jumped on the social media bandwagon, either always plugged into her phone or on it. "Malia, your sister's talking to you!?" This was the usual response from Mum; "Malia seriously I'll take that thing off you in a minute."

"Sorry Mum, what?"

"It's pardon Mal. Your sister has been asking you for the past five minutes how your day was!" Mum wasn't impressed but it was just typical Malia. In ways all you could do was laugh; she had her own little content bubble even if it made no sense to anyone else. At least she'd be safe from the romance dramas that happened in the real world. "Sorry sis, yeh good thanks. How was lunch?" At this I looked at Mum, not only surprised that she'd remembered our plans but also to get a sign on how to respond. Luckily Mum jumped to my rescue "It was ok, interesting, but ok." By this time Malia had gone back to her phone totally oblivious to the response.

The evening was pretty standard. Malia stayed attached to her phone, Mum glued herself to the soaps and Dad, well he just plugged himself into his laptop to drown out the so called 'trash' that Mum was watching. I, on the other hand, sat in the corner of our sofa and thought. I sometimes referred to my life as something out of the movies, but not the lovey dovey Disney kind but more the romantic comedies that ended badly. Something along the lines of Titanic but maybe not so dramatic. The sad part is that my love life really was that shocking, I couldn't make it up if I wanted to. It had started and ended with Adam and just when I thought moving on was finally about to happen he appeared again. Even though I could think of nothing better than shaking him off once and for all, part of me questioned whether I really wanted to. Deep down the feelings were still there, that was clearly evident from the impact he still had on me. He was bad news, I knew that, but it was telling my heart that was what I was failing at. If my so far love mishap wasn't written for the movies then I don't know what its purpose was because I certainly couldn't see any benefits from where I was sitting.

SJ

All night I sat there expecting some backlash from my embarrassing encounter earlier that day, instead I got nothing. I got the normal 'how was your day' from my father as he got in from work, I got the usual silent treatment from Malia, as we all did, and got the small talk from Mum about Eastenders latest storyline. Everything seemed strangely normal. In a way, I wanted it over and done with so I could move on. I hated walking on eggshells, never aware of when the telling off could occur but for tonight I could do with the peace and quiet.

There was the usual Queen Vic drama being broadcasted in front of us. There was something about soaps that made your own life seem hassle free, almost simple, but today even they couldn't make mine seem normal. My phone suddenly starting buzzing on the sofa, not only jarring my mum but also attracting the attention of my sister. Malia gave me that glare telling me to answer it. Seeing the name on the screen made me freeze, the phone still ringing out its dulcet tones in my hand. "Kass, I can't hear the TV."

"Sorry Mum" and with that I turned the phone to mute. I don't know why but it seemed the only reasonable thing to do. Why would Senna be phoning me if it wasn't to advise me of his disappointment. He didn't have time to reply to a quick message earlier so why bother now? Maybe it was just to rub the embarrassment in even more; something I certainly didn't need. I had flaws, yes, but I didn't need any man to tell me them. I felt it was better for me to never speak to him again rather than going through the pain of really knowing what he thought of me. Before I could reassure myself of my decision my phone screen lit up again, Senna's name brightening up the front. OK, so he really wanted me to know what an idiot I was. Had I not gone through enough without the hottest most mysterious guy I had ever met needing to tell me? I was tempted to answer; the day couldn't get any worse after all; then on second thought maybe it could so with that I turned the phone over, curled up further into my snuggle blanket and concentrated on the TV ahead.

My concentration lasted all of two seconds. My mind kept wondering to the whys and whats of what Senna and mine's conversation could have been. In my head it would have gone something like "I'm sorry Kass, please don't let him get between us" but the most likely outcome would have probably gone "Kass how could you? He's family and you're just a little kid." Ouch. The thought of it made me flinch, but the truthfulness of it hurt the most. Maybe he did see me as a kid; yes I was eighteen but my actions today were unjustified even for my thirteen year old sister let alone me. It was the last thing I remember thinking about.

"Kass."

I felt a shove on my arm. It then occurred to me that I

must have drifted off. The room was bright, unusual for night time. I focused my eyes, seeing my Mum standing over me. She still appeared blurred but I could still work out that she was in different clothes. The room stood quiet.

"Kass are you ok? We did try and wake you to get you to bed but you were fast off. You looked too peaceful to move."

So I'd stayed here all night; no wonder my back didn't seem to want to work. A night on the sofa probably wasn't the brightest idea for someone with a bad back. Without saying anything more Mum helped me sit up, but not without the flinches, and handed me an orange juice. Casting aside the fact that I'd just slept on a leather sofa for ten or so hours, I actually felt rather refreshed. Mum was still staring at me, more like giving me the once over, so I guessed I should say something.

"Hi Mum." Typical me. I didn't know what to say so I stuck with something safe, something I knew could not get misinterpreted in anyway and something that was as least embarrassing as possible. The receiving look on her face was a picture but in the end she knew better than to question my reply. Glancing at the clock, it must have been quite late. I was prone to sleeping in late but from Mum's expression this seemed late even for me.

"Kass you know need to get up. Someone's coming round to see you." That's when it all came back to me; all the events from the day before and the dreaded phone calls that I deliberately ignored. Surely Mum wouldn't do that to me. She obviously read my anxiety, "Kass, why the face? I thought it'd be nice to see Lottie. You've seemed a tad down the past few days so some girly time will do you good. Now go, get ready." That one name made the day seem brighter already. My Mum really did know me; some girly time was just what I needed. Removing myself from the sofa, surprised not to see my imprint left behind, I let out a huge sigh of relief. For a moment then my heart actually stopped; the thought of even being in the same room of Tattoo Man again made me feel physically sick. He clearly was going to influence me for a while much to my dismay.

If there was anyone to detract my fascination it was Lottie. She had such a relaxed approach to men seeing them as lessons and experiences rather than knocks to the ego. I was embarrassed though; not only of my actions but also of the way I got so easily drawn in. I kept trying to remember even the smallest of details to reassure me that I did know something about this man and not just the shape of his abs or the distinct smell of his aftershave. I knew he had tattoos and I knew he was Adam's cousin but apart from that my mind was blank. Surely, he'd told me things about him the other night, but it was now evident my attraction was merely physical, something that was harder to shift than actual feelings. Shaking my head, in the hope to push those doomed feelings aside, I started to undress from my pyjamas and stepped into the shower. The water was warm, much warmer than I'd expected. I was always one to enjoy a roasting shower, the kind where you could just let your imagination run; the kind that took you to a tropical waterfall location. The burning sensation was once again welcomed but this time in the hope to loosen my muscles from a night on the sofa rather than the after effects of a rain downpour.

For what seemed like ten minutes I managed to think of everything but Senna Jackson; the weather, the summer months and the crew. If there was anything that could put all these tense and frustrating feelings to bed it was them. My friends were always used to me being their shoulder to cry on; I was the strong one, the go to girl but now I was going to need them more than ever. Maybe I was overthinking everything; maybe yesterday wasn't as bad as it first seemed, maybe Adam and I could be friends and maybe Tattoo Man shared similar feelings to mine. Then again, was that what I wanted? Part of me would love for all of this to disappear especially all the hatred I felt towards to Adam, but then again that hatred was the reason I had become so strong these past months. Yes, Adam had left me a heartbroken girl but he'd also made me the independent woman I was today. Thanking him would be very undeserved but in a way, he did me a favour. There was the other part of me that wished Adam, Senna and the Jackson family never existed. Even though Bob Jackson was one of the nicest men of our neighbourhood, his son seemed to have missed all the gentlemen lessons, and instead just wooed girls with his tattoos and sexy charm. Senna certainly wasn't his father's son; then again it was me that ignored him last night and it was me that wasted wine on him.

I'd been standing in the bathroom, wrapped in just a towel, for what seemed like eternity. It wasn't until a knock on the door came from outside until I realised just how long.
"Kass are you ok? Lottie's here."
Shit, Lottie.
"Sorry Mum, yes I'm fine. I'll be down in two."
Normally I wouldn't be seen with no makeup or my hair a mess, but Lottie wouldn't mind. She was the last person that would judge. She knew me inside out and for the first time in hours I felt normal. I chucked some warm clothes on, gave my hair one last rub then made my way downstairs.
"If you feel as rough as you look, thank god I've come to the rescue." Oh, she knew how to cheer me up straight away.
"Hi to you too Lottie." She stood up gave me a big hug and helped herself to the biscuits my Mum had put on the table. Lottie was welcome any time and she knew it. She'd make herself at home, have in depth conversations with my parents and would pop round even though she knew I wasn't in. Lottie was a gem and right now she knew she had to work some magic.

"So, there's a guy, right? And how come I have to hear this second hand Kass? Bet even the guys knew before me?" She was right. Nate had been told before her but in my defence they were there at The Baggers whilst she was off chatting up anyone that would listen. She came across quite harshly but I knew she meant well. She was trying to brighten the mood and soon moved on to demanding all the details.

"So a name? Age? Occupation.?..." The list went on and it was like a mother's inquisition. I told her all about Senna. I told her all about lunch at The Swallow and I told her all about the phone calls I purposefully declined. Her response was expected; a huge laughing fit that seemed to go on for minutes then a simple "Oh Kass." I knew what was coming next "Kass, what have I told you about men. You can't give them the power but don't worry we'll fix this. You just need a good night out." My Mum suddenly appeared in the doorway but it was pretty obvious she had heard the whole conversation.

Her presence hadn't come unnoticed "That's ok isn't Mrs G?" For some reason Lottie always felt the need to ask my mother when she was planning something. It was the one thing I never understood about Lottie, the need to be liked and accepted. She was one of the most down to earth people I knew yet struggled with making long term relationships whether they be friendly or romantically.

"Lottie that sounds like an excellent idea. Kass there's plenty of fish in the sea. Just have some fun instead of acting ten years older than what you are."

My Mum was right, as usual. I had a tendency of planning ahead instead of living the here and now. The best way of getting Adam and Senna out of my head was to physically move on and with Lottie in charge she wouldn't call it a night until that was accomplished. Finally, the conversation moved on from my lack of a love life to a more promising topic, one in which I actually succeeded. Originally university was something I was never interested in, despite my encouraging grades and ambition, much to the frustration of teachers and friends. For months I would hear "but you have a gift, it would be a waste not to go" or "I wish I could get your grades" but for me, further education seemed un-enthralling compared to actually putting my knowledge into use. Lottie, on the other hand, was bright but the least motivated person I knew. Since turning eighteen a few months ago it was all about the parties, all about being known. It wasn't really my scene but she was my number one girl and sometimes compromising was all I could do. Someone had to keep an eye on her anyhow. She was clearly dreading results day but in typical Lottie style she tried to remain positive. I, on the other hand, didn't feel nervous or excited. In fact it was just another day with just a few more marks on a piece of paper. In the end I accepted university as the next step, choosing a course at Manchester; I just wasn't about to waste the summer with excitement when I was leaving everyone I loved behind.

Lottie and I sat there for hours talking about anything but boys. She was the best distraction anyone could ask for. My sister had come in from school, my Dad from work and Lottie was still there talking away. Getting a word in edge ways was hard but her conversation was appreciated. She ended up staying for dinner asking my Mum what we were having, and after the reply of homemade lasagne, gently invited herself to stay. It was gone nine before Lottie excused herself and went home. I felt mentally exhausted. Lottie was full on but today she seemed determined to make me feel better. Not only had we arranged a wild night out but had several plans on how to spend our summer. I felt better but more importantly I felt like my feelings and actions were normal. After thanking Lottie, giving her a hug and walking her to her car I went back inside to thank my Mum. She was standing in the kitchen talking to Dad. "You look happier" she said before I could even find the words to thank her. A hug seemed more appropriate than a response. I hugged her hard and soon it turned into a Green family hug, with my Dad joining in then to everyone's amazement, Malia too. It was an unusual moment but one that showed how strong we were. It was just us four. Our family wasn't disjointed like Lottie's where throughout her entire childhood she was tossed between her mum's and dad's houses. My Mum and Dad were seen as unique, making their relationship something that Mal and I longed for.

I went to bed a lot happier. Not only were there fresh sheets on my bed but there were no more phone calls to dodge and I truly did have the greatest friends a girl could ask for. Things finally seemed on the up and with a little help and encouragement from my crew, I could start calling the last few days a blip. Part of me still saw this as wishful thinking but we all deserved a little luck every now and again. Before jumping into bed I gave myself one final look over in the mirror. After the recent events of the past week it seemed only apt to give myself a telling off "Kass you're an idiot. Get your shit together." It was probably a pointless task, as at eighteen years old, I'm sure there was plenty more stupidity to come; still, it made me feel better.

Before drifting off to sleep I tried some of the meditation techniques I'd read about in Glamour magazine. From the quarter lotus to the Burmese position I went, remembering something about breathing being the most important factor. It was a mind boggle to me; yet between the tangling of legs and arms and the soothing whale music echoing around my bedroom, I started to feel my inner zen (*whatever that may be*). It was a peace that undoubtedly would have disappeared by the morning but maybe that was just me being pessimistic all again. Maybe things were about to change for the better and with that I unfolded out of my lotus and let my head hit the pillow. My hard mattress was a welcoming relief to my back after the previous night. Turning off my light switch I gazed up at the glow in the dark stars that still remained on my ceiling from years ago and tried to focus on the music that surrounded me. The whale music was beautiful and strong; and with that I drifted off into a surprisingly deep sleep.

By the following morning the music was still playing, even if significantly quieter, either that or my mind was singing it to one's self. My inner zen was clearly important to someone. Going over to my laptop to reassure my sanity, I caught sight of myself in the mirror. Unlike previous viewings my face seemed brighter, my freckles more pronounced and my eyes seem to have some of their old sparkle back. Maybe these magazines really did know the ins and outs to ' a more relaxing you.' Combined with the generous amount of sleep, I felt like an almost complete Kassia Green again. The sun shone brightly through my curtains as if to agree with my observation, causing an automatic smile to appear across my face. Maybe a little optimism never hurt no one and with that I paused the whales and pulled on my dressing gown before heading off to show Mum the old, happy me.

I found her sitting on the breakfast stalls, her back to me, talking to Maggie. Surely it wasn't late enough for visitors yet again we were used to Maggie just popping in after her morning commute to the butchers. She'd often bring back the finest of meat packs, one for her and one for us, and then there would always be a steak chop for me. I used to love Maggie coming round and even with my inner relaxation still in full swing, I couldn't help but wish she wasn't here. Deep down I knew she wouldn't avoid the house for long, and to Maggie and my Mum a few days without seeing each other would equate to hours of talking to catch up on all the gossip. Their friendship reminded me a lot of my friendship group's.

Lottie and Harry loved to know everyone else's business and almost made it their mission to do so. Even the thought of them stalking someone's social media accounts was enough to make you laugh. I did so inwardly.

I couldn't help but hide and listen from behind the door, not only in the hope to find out some information but also to prolong the agony of Maggie's awkward hello. Senna was her son, Adam her nephew; they had a family connection that even their wrong doings couldn't break. I heard the voices suddenly stop as if they'd heard my presence. That was the thing about mums; they knew things even went they couldn't see them. Entering the kitchen I could feel myself hold my breathe. There was something about seeing Maggie again that scared me; that look of disappointment. Mum turned round. "Kass," she seemed actually surprised to see me. "How come you're up so early. I don't know how you got any sleep with that music blaring!" So it was Mum that turned it down. That explained things I guess.

"Sorry Mum if it kept you awake, I was trying to relax, find my inner zen." I couldn't help but look semi-smug with my reference. Mum seemed intrigued herself "your inner zen Kass?" Explaining my optimism was pointless so I just nodded and embraced the moment to say hi to Maggie. She appeared her usual, bright and cheery self; wearing her bright pink running gear paired with a matching lip shade. This was Maggie all over. She was the light to everyone's dark.

"Hi Maggie." She looked straight at me and for a moment I thought a back hand was coming my way. Instead she stood up, gave me the once over before squeezing me hard. Instantly I relaxed. "Oh Kass, what have my boys done to you?" I knew Senna was actually hers but to hear her label Adam with the same brush was hard to hear. How could such a heartless man be related to such a caring and thoughtful woman? Nonetheless it was a relief, not only because I needed her to like me but I also knew how much Maggie's opinion of me meant to my mother. I didn't want sides to be made, I didn't expect her to choose but it seemed like even she wasn't happy about the certain situation.

I couldn't find the words to say so I simply replied with a "thank you" and hugged her back a little bit tighter. Mum's eyes seemed to be staring a whole in my back. Letting go of my grip I turned round to see her standing up with a huge grin on her face.
"And what makes you so happy?" I asked.
"Can't a girl be happy to see her best friend and elder daughter sharing a hug? I now know if anything ever happened to me, my two girls would still have a mother."
"Mum what kind of thought is that!?"
"I'm sorry darling but I could choke on this piece of toast right now" and with that she took a bite of the last slice of toast that I'm pretty sure was left for me.

Something started vibrating in my dressing gown pocket. Pulling my phone out I noticed the screen flash with Lottie's name. I sat and stared at the phone for what seemed like minutes waiting for my voicemail cut in. I was too embraced in an adult conversation to have a flamboyant conversation with my own bestie before midday. My Mum had seen the caller ID, "take it Kass." Her voice was calm yet it seemed like an order. Like usual she was probably right. How could I ignore her after everything she did for me yesterday. I had felt like a new person since she left last night. Excusing myself I accepted the call and headed off for a trek down the garden. The sun was making an appearance through the clouds and birds were singing at large. "Hi Lottie" "Kass, what happened to picking up the phone straight away!" She really had turned into a demanding and bossy person but I loved her nonetheless.

"Sorry, what's up?" A blackbird was perched on the fence ahead. In typical Kassia fashion, I became transfixed in its music rather than listening to the rant of Lottie on the other end of the phone. I came attuned to the melody of the bird's song and closed my eyes to try and find that peace from last night. It wasn't until Lottie was screaming names at me that I started to concentrate. Usually I'd just let her shout to get it off her chest, but there seemed to be something different about her voice that made me want to listen.
"Harrison!"
"Nate!"
"Kieran!" and then there was that name.
"Senna!"

Why was Lottie shouting their names at me in the same sentence? They didn't know each other so it was hardly in a friendly context.

"Lottie, slow down. Start again" and with that I sat down on the decking, with my back to the bird, and started to focus. I listened to her explain the scenario, one that I wish would never happen. Whether it happened exactly how Lottie mentioned was hard to tell; she often had a tendency at exaggerating the truth. She went on to describe how Harrison, Nate and Kieran had gone to the Swallow yesterday to walk Kieran's dog, Polly. That was enough; I could see where this was heading. I didn't want to know but my ears just wouldn't shut off. They were walking round the grounds when they bumped into Senna and Adam talking outside. I stopped Lottie there "Lottie, just stop. I don't want to know."

Senna had been nothing but nice to me. He didn't lead me on, I just let my heart be dragged in to his friendly charm and then ignore a text; no real biggy. Ironically, I hated my friends for protecting me. Did they always have to make my love life into aggressive brawls? They were as soft as anything until it came to someone upsetting me. Frequently I'd told them that I was strong enough to protect myself but they just wouldn't have it, and rightly so. I fell for guys too quickly, it was that simple. All it took was me looking down or posting a slightly depressing Facebook status and they'd be on my case, Harrison more so, wanting to know all the details.

He couldn't just politely ask someone to leave me alone but instead made verbal threats and then legged it so not to get in trouble. In typical Harry manner, I was left to deal with the fallout afterwards. I'd have to go around apologising to all relevant parties and face the disapproving look from my mother. She still loved them, I knew that, but something told me that she wasn't to be as accommodating over this situation.

It wasn't until my Mum came to join me that I noticed the blackbird's song had stopped and the clouds had dispersed. The sun was now hot and blinding my eyes.

"Darling what's wrong?" She didn't wait for an answer but instead moulded herself round me and hugged me tight. There really was nothing like a mother's touch. I didn't want to explain what was wrong but I knew I'd have to eventually. Still, I buried my face further into my knees waiting for the tears to dry out. After years of crying over Adam I was surprised I had any more left in me but then again anything was possible these past few days. Why couldn't everything go back to the way things were a week ago? I would have been in college ready for double maths with Mr Logan, with me finally being over Adam and looking forward to the summer ahead. Instead I was a mess. We were all so ready to embrace adulthood but instead I sat here now wishing I could turn back the clock 10 years to when life and feelings were simple.

"Kass, come on speak to me." I knew I couldn't avoid the conversation forever so I sat up and wiped the few last remaining tears to see her looking at me. She looked generally worried, her usual happier persona from earlier gone. Taking one deep breathe I went on to explain the situation whilst focusing on our surroundings rather than her facial expressions. That was the thing with my Mum, and supposedly all of us Green's, our faces expressed exactly how we were feeling. There were no hiding emotions even if we tried our hardest. It was through the Adam saga that I realised this, so lately I'd just stopped trying. Even though I felt let down by the boys and Lottie, I couldn't help but stick up for them with my Mum going on to explain how they were only trying to protect me. They were idiots but their intentions were good; still it hurt. When I'd stopped, I closed my eyes trying to find that inner calmness from last night, before focusing on Mum's face. For once in my life I couldn't read it. Was she angry? Upset? Or worst of all disappointed?

"Mum say something," I longed for a reassuring response but all I got was "and how do you feel?" It was a stab to the heart. It was an emotionless response. How did I feel? I paused trying to find the right words to say exactly how I felt but I couldn't. I'm sure she wasn't just talking about the whole Harrison thing but instead my feelings towards Senna and that was something I really didn't know. I looked at her straight in the eyes and said one word in hope that she'd understand "Adam." She closed her eyes, let out a deep sigh then gave me one last squeeze before walking back up the garden to where Maggie was standing.

Mum reached Maggie and almost collapsed in her arms. She was clearly disappointed, I just don't know who at. It was painful to watch but I couldn't look away. I'd been a complete nightmare the past few days, something that must have pained Mum to watch, and this latest ordeal just seemed one step too far. She'd find herself apologising to Maggie for something that wasn't her fault. Contemplating whether to move or just watch, I tried to focus on my breathing. It seemed to relax after a few moments and just like that I was being serenaded again by the blackbird. The melody was striking and far from the whale music I fell asleep to last night yet it still provided some comfort.

I needed to speak to Mum, to Maggie, to try and fix this new mess but most of all I needed to speak to Senna. He probably hated me, thinking he was the victim of my abhorrence. The sun was still beaming down as I made my way up towards the house. The sun was making the slightly overgrowing grass glow as the lengthy strands brushed round my ankles. Weather wise it was to be a scorcher but something told me that the Green/Jackson households were to experience something of a storm.

Maggie saw me first, letting go of Mum and storming straight over to me. "Kass what have you said to your friends!? I know he can be a twat but he doesn't deserve to be assaulted at work!" Understandably she was angry but this wasn't my fault. I didn't know where to look or what to say and this time it didn't look like I had Mum's backing. She was ashamed and looked just as disappointed as Maggie. I could have offered Harrison to come round to explain his actions but on second thought I don't know what good that would have done. He was my friend so ultimately the book stopped at me. Maggie's friendly character from earlier had disappeared with her eagle eyes and dramatic eyebrows suggesting that she'd love to punch me back.

"Mags, I know you're angry at me but I promise I had nothing to do with it. I have nothing against your son, more like the exact opposite." I could see my words collating in her head, her trying to figure out exactly what I meant. She forgave me over throwing wine over her son but this seemed more like a personal attack, one that was intentional. I needed Mum on side, I needed her to protect me.

Mum was nowhere to be seen and still Maggie stood broad in front of me. I'd never witnessed this scary side of Maggie before. I didn't know what to say or what to do so I just stood there looking at her. I felt embarrassed and my body language reflected it. My shoulders were slumped and my eyes still teary. It was taking all of my energy to stop the tears from flowing again. "Kass" she said, this time more calmingly, "come here" and with that she held my hand and led me over to the patio chairs. The atmosphere had seemed to have settled whilst Maggie sat there sighing heavily. We sat in silence for a few minutes before she spoke again, "Kass, I know this is going to seem harsh but I need you to stay away from my son and his cousin."

She paused as if to allow me to take in her words. Staying away from Adam was easy, Senna on the other hand may be a little trickier. I knew it was what needed to happen to protect my heart. I hadn't truly fallen for Senna but he was certainly someone who had caught my attention.

Maggie hadn't finished, "I know this is not your fault but I saw what Adam did to you and I can't be semi-responsible for my son doing the same to you." I couldn't quite believe what she was saying. Was Maggie on my side? Was she really just trying to protect me? "Maggie what do you mean? Senna hasn't done anything to me."

"I know darling but he will. He messes with girl's emotions; not on purpose but he's a heartbreaker. I've tried my best with him, I really have, but for some reason he still hasn't learnt the concept of a loving two-way relationship. Don't get me wrong, you'd be the perfect girl for him and I wouldn't be happier. I just couldn't forgive myself if he was to hurt you or if I had to see your Mum upset again. It broke her you know, not knowing how to make you feel better. It's our job to protect our children and she felt like she failed." It was hard to hear. I had never thought about how my depressive state affected my Mum. She was always a strong person, someone that seemed capable of carrying everyone but now it seemed Maggie was right, all possible feelings for Senna to be buried.

"Ok Maggie." It's all I could say and with that she gave me a quick hug before getting out her mobile. I left her alone and set off to find Mum.

I found her in the living room also on the phone. She seemed to pause when she saw me; I flashed her a tentative smile before leaving her to it. Getting Mum on side again appeared to be a slightly bigger challenge than Maggie. I trekked back upstairs and left the proper adults to their individual conversations. My inner zen had completely disappeared, me feeling tenser than ever. With that I walked straight over to my laptop and restarted my whale music from earlier. Climbing onto my bed I moved my cushions to allow enough room for me to enter the quarter lotus move yet again. My wall clock was only just clicking to eleven o'clock and I already felt emotionally exhausted. Focusing on the soothing tones that filled the room, I started to loosen up. I tried to direct my mind to everything other than the recent episodes of my life. I drifted off to our up and coming family holiday to Mexico, trying to create a mental list of what still needed buying; from bikinis to dresses and heels to sandals. I may not be feeling the most glamourous but no one knew me in Mexico hence making it my aim to impress. August couldn't come sooner but for now, with the help of my whales, I was to take one day at a time staying as relaxed as possible.

Remaining calm was something I didn't know a lot about; I liked to know what was going on and when I didn't I panicked, over thought things and then unsurprisingly acted like some crazy, weird lady. It was just who I was. Some would call it irrational, somewhat psychotic behaviour, I'd just call it the result of years of standing on egg shells. Adam Jackson would do that to you; it was hard knowing his next move, whether it be to leave or a spontaneous romantic gesture, but either way it would have you thinking why. Now it appeared that Senna Jackson was to be a somewhat similar specie. I'd missed a bullet and that was something to celebrate. Maggie had saved me from a prolonged heartbreak and for that I was entirely grateful.

Fighting the devil

A knock at the door startled me. The whale music had now turned into a majestic waterfall, making my bladder adjust. I wiggled myself out of the lotus and took in my current surroundings once more. There I was, back in the real world, sat on my bed within my four bedroom walls. Mum came walking in, not choosing to wait for my reply. She looked a little happier to see me yet her usually tanned face seemed somewhat ghost-like. Had she been crying or was she really just pale today? I opted for the first explanation; "Mum's what's up?" Without saying a word she climbed up on the bed next to me. It was now my turn to do the hugging, something that she seemed to appreciate.

I let her hug me back tightly before pushing for an answer again, "Is everything ok?" Mum was normally the strong one, the one that held me together but now she seemed far from her usual self. She gave me one last squeeze before parting herself from me. I looked at her face and it already seemed brighter, cheerier, than it did five minutes ago.

"Don't worry about me darling, I'm ok if you are. Remember Mum's feel every emotion their children do if not more so." And just like that I knew exactly what was up. I felt emotionally exhausted, meaning she did too. Every tear I'd shed, she had too and all that bottled up hatred I felt towards Adam was inside her too. Even parent's needed a hug and comfort every now and again. Part of me lit up with the thought of being a little less alone, the other part of me was overwhelmed with guilt to put Mum through all of this. When would I stop falling for the wrong men?

"Mum, I'm sorry."
"Oh Kass," she stroked my hair like she did when I was little "…you have nothing to be sorry for. Yes you're a tad hard work at times but I wouldn't have it any other way. You keep your old mother young!" She was clearly trying to lighten the mood but it didn't melt the guilt away. All I could do was look at her, trying to see the damage my stresses had caused her. Truth is Mum could be 10 years younger; her and Maggie always had looked after their skin going on monthly facials and only using Clarins.

"Come on Kass, cheer up! Now I must go back to Maggie." She climbed up off the bed and opened the door. "Sort yourself out then come and join us. Oh and Kass, you deserve 10 times better than both Adam and Senna. You remember that." Mum's words couldn't make me light up more if they tried. I totally forgot that Maggie was still downstairs, and my conversation with

Lottie. I hated falling out with her but I couldn't help but feel let down, not just by her but the guys too. Mum left the room a lot happier than she entered; she was right it was time I cheered up. Grabbing my hairbrush off the side, I gave my long red hair a quick comb. It's normal shine had disappeared these last few days so I ran some coconut oil through the ends, gave my head a quick shake and went downstairs.

"My favourite girls! What took you so long? Kass you need to learn to share your mother sometimes." I knew she was joking. She was right though; Mum needed some fun rather than always picking up the pieces of my broken heart.

"Sorry Maggie, she's all yours." I tried to sound upbeat but I couldn't face dealing with any more emotional outbursts alone. It wasn't as if I wanted anymore but heartbreak seemed to have a way of following me around and something told me it was still firmly on my tracks. Mum quickly sat down next to Maggie and their conversation swiftly carried on from where they left off. They really were like a pair of teenagers, none stop talking, yet their friendship was refreshing. I was so much like my Mum and Lottie, Maggie. That reminded me; I should probably phone Lottie back, say my piece and clear the air. I always was taught dwelling on something never fixed anything.

The sun was properly shining now; the blackbirds into full swing, practising their tuning. I positioned my head up to the sky and let my face absorb the sun beams.

The sun was properly shining now; the blackbirds into full swing, practising their tuning. I positioned my head up to the sky and let my face absorb the sun beams. All my tenseness just floated away. Getting back to the real world, I grabbed my iPhone from my dressing gown pocket and found Lottie's number. She picked up straight way; typical Lottie really. Her phone was always glued to her side, day or night, yet her reasoning why was always one that baffled me. "What if I miss Harry's message Kass?" Harry was no other than Prince Harry, convinced that after meeting him once and shouting her number out to him he a) heard it and b) was going to use it. Still, I could never fault the girl for trying.

"Kass, I'm so sor…"
"Lottie, just stop! Let me talk for once and actually try to listen." I was shocked at my own aggression but in all the years I've known Lottie no one had ever put her in her place. She would talk for England if you let her, often overriding everyone else. Usually I didn't mind but for some reason I was fired up and had to get it off my chest. "Lottie I told you all of that because I trusted you. You know what the boys are like, you knew what would happen and you knew the trouble I would get in and you still did it. Why couldn't you just keep your big gob shut for once? Why did you have to go running off to Harrison? If I wanted him to know the ins and outs of my feelings do you not thing I would tell him?" I couldn't help but smile; I'd never questioned Lottie before.

"No." The response was short, blunt and very un-Lottie like. No to what part? I didn't often get a word in edge ways but when I did Lottie never disagreed. "What do you mean no?"

"Kass no you wouldn't have gone to Harry. You know how he feels about you. For years all he's done is try to protect you, push aside his own feelings for you. You've been selfish Kass. He was there all through Adam and he'll be here all through Senna. I'm sorry you feel let down but I won't apologise for telling him. You want to be loved Kass? Try looking a bit closer to home, I don't think anyone will love you or want to protect you more than him." The line went silent. I couldn't find the words for a reply as I tried to contemplate every word she had just said. Truth is I knew how Harry felt but I thought we'd sorted it. We were to remain at just best friends, the one that I could always rely on. Maybe I had relied on him too much, given him too many signals. My mind wandered back to all those times I had cried on him, said I needed him. I couldn't help but feel bad; my insides were turning and I felt physically sick. The pain I felt now was what Harry had been feeling for years. How had I not picked up on how he was still feeling? He had been my hero, my rock through all of Adam. He'd saved me more times than I could recall and I'd taken it for granted.

My phone was still in my hand. The whispered calls of "Kass, Kass" could be heard as I dropped it to the ground. I didn't pick it up but instead stared at it until the call cut off. Lottie was right; I had no right being angry at any of them. Harrison had tried to help me in the only way he knew possible. Who could blame him with all those unwanted emotions boiling up inside him? I saw Harrison more like a brother, something I'd told him on more than one occasion. It had always been said as a compliment but I can imagine it was probably like being stabbed in the heart time after time. I was meant to be his best mate, the one that made him laugh not cry. My mind went into overdrive. Was there a way back from this? Could I just forget what Lottie had said or would I need to say something? Part of me even contemplated seeing him as more than a brother, the other tried seeing my life without him in it. It was then that the tears got harder, so much so it was getting hard to breathe. Truth is, Harrison was part of me; he'd been my third arm for so long, not having there was unbearable.

I was aware Mum and Maggie were watching from the kitchen window, still it didn't stop the tears from flowing. My chest was hurting and my legs were numb. I thought I had experience heartache from Adam, and more recently Senna, but this pain was so much more. Harrison meant more. Everything he'd ever done was out of love. Everything he'd ever said was out of love. He knew all my flaws; had seen me in my worst state and still stood by my side. Lottie was right; I was selfish. I'd ignored his feelings because I needed him. Maybe it would be best if I let him go. I eventually fell to ground, clutching my chest and that was the last thing I remember thinking. Harrison was better off with a new best friend, one he wasn't in love with.

Through pierced eyes, the lights were bright and blinding. I felt suffocated and as I tried to move I felt restrained. From what I could make out, things were moving around me and there were distant voices. One seemed to be Mum, the other Maggie and the other I was unsure of. I forced myself to open my eyes to establish my surroundings. There were machines and doctors. Hospital it was then. Why was I here? The conversation with Lottie was crystal clear, the feelings I felt afterwards were still raw but hospital seemed a bit extreme. I remember thinking Harrison would be better off without me but had I done something stupid? Had I really meant it? I tried shouting Mum, but the oxygen mask made it a pathetic attempt. I tried again but still she was engrossed in conversation with Maggie and a dark, tall man that I could only assume was my doctor. Instead of a third attempt I just closed my eyes and tried to figure the answers out for myself. Every scenario went through my head, from a heart attack to deliberately trying to hurt myself but I laid here feeling fine. Nothing was physically broken; I checked all my limbs were in working condition, wiggling my feet, my hips and my hands. Left hand was fine, right hand was…someone was holding it. They certainly weren't there before. I didn't need to know who just yet. I laid there pretending to sleep, appreciating the touch.

"Kass. Kass can you hear me?" It wasn't Mum's voice, it wasn't even Maggie's. I didn't need to open my eyes to know who it was. Tattoo Man. What was he doing here? Obviously, Maggie had told him but after getting punched because of me I was surprised he was still bothered. Still, his voice was soothing and for a second I forgot about the heartache that had got me in this place. There was a second voice "Darling open your eyes for me." Mum. She sounded so worried. I found myself relaying all the times I'd lent on her, all the tears she'd seen me cry and the amount of times I'd indirectly upset her. Tears felt like they wanted to escape. I clenched my eyes tighter and tighter to stop them. They clearly knew I was awake, "Kass, everything's ok. We're here. Please open your eyes." Mum's voice was broken. I couldn't see her upset anymore so one by one I opened my eyes. Her face was the first thing I saw; her eyes red raw and it was clear she'd been crying. I didn't mean to make her upset but no matter what I did, she was always affected. I had not only failed at being a best friend but also a daughter. The hurt was too much. Machines starting beeping and the room became black. I wanted to scream but I couldn't find the words. The pain was pulling me down a black hole, one I was struggling to climb out of.

I don't know how long I'd been out cold. My surroundings were different when I came around; the room was dark but I could still make out my company was the same. Mum was scrunched up in one armchair next to the bed, Senna in the other. They couldn't have been comfortable. I knew for a fact Mum loved nothing more than her big bed and piles of pillows. The chair carried everything but the same pleasure. Seeing them both here made me smile. Mum looked so peaceful and I wouldn't blame her for dreaming about a simpler life; Senna would make me smile no matter where he was. He had that automatic look that drew you in but ironically that's why I was here in the first place. I should be mad at him for even existing, for accidentally hurting Harrison again, but I couldn't find it in me. All the traces of hatred in my body were aimed towards me at the moment and believe me, that was exhausting enough. I didn't have it in me to wake them so instead just watched. Their chests moved up and down, and whenever it looked like they were stirring I closed my eyes. For now the peace and quiet of night-time was much more appealing than the questions that were bound to follow.

My arm was being prodded. Hard. My eyes opened in an instance. I was taken back by the face that stood over me. It wasn't one I recognised. His eyes were tiny but it was his nose that made me laugh. It overtook his face. "She's awake. Senna she's awake. Darling Mummy's here." Mum always did have to treat me like a baby when I was ill. The doctor stepped back to give me the once over. He took out the flipchart at the end of my bed and started taking notes. "Mrs Green, you're daughter seems on the mend." He looked up, "Hi Kassia, I'm Dr Johnson. Your Mum and boyfriend haven't left your side all week." Wait, my boyfriend? What Senna? And all week? I'd been here all week. Why what was wrong with me? "You had a series of panic attacks, a kind we don't often see. Have you been under any stress lately?" Before I could find the energy to remove my oxygen mask and answer, my Mum was already talking. "Does a broken heart count Dr? And just for the record that guy certainly isn't my daughter's boyfriend." If looks could kill, Senna would be ten feet under right now. I thought Mum liked Senna, how could she not being Maggie's son. The rest of the conversation was a blur, with me drifting in and out of it as my body allowed.

Being in hospital was exhausting, either that or they had me on some pretty strong stuff. I was in here for panic attacks, could I really be any lamer if I tried? I'd let myself fall for two people that were no good and now this. Pathetic Kass, just pathetic. I wondered if the group knew I was here, whether they had bothered to ask about my health. All these things started flying through my head but I kept coming up with the same emotion. I was in a hospital surrounded by other patients and two people who clearly cared yet I felt so alone. It was as if I needed my third arm, I needed to see Harrison and with that I opened my eyes.

"Mum?" My mouth was so dry and my voice hoarse. She was still in conversation with Dr Johnson, completely ignoring Senna's presence. If it was under other circumstances the tension would seem odd but in ways I could relate to Mum's annoyance.

"Mum!" I tried a little harder to grab her attention, so much so I started coughing. The cough was tight and hurt my whole chest. Senna grabbed me some water. I couldn't down it soon enough; the liquid was so refreshing and the pain was instantly soothed. "Mum?"
"Kass, it's ok. Rest your voice."
"No Mum, I need to ask you something."
"Anything darling, what's up?"
"Has Harrison been in touch? I need to speak to him."
"Oh Kass, what's happened between you two? I knew he must have had something to do with all of this. Lottie told me you two had a row about him."
"Mum has he asked about me?"
"No darling. I haven't heard from him, just Lottie."
The words hit hard. I knew the chances were that Lottie had been relaying all the latest gossip of my embarrassing hospital visit to him but I still expected him to visit. I couldn't just lay there with him thinking I didn't care or appreciate him. My mobile was resting on the side table. Should I contact him? Maybe he'd messaged me directly instead. Yes, that was probably it. I probably had hundreds of messages waiting for me. In an instance, I grabbed my iPhone from beside me. Ouch. A pain in my side ran through my body with such force I couldn't help but let out a little screech. Mum was the first to worry, quickly racing to my side with a worried look on her face.

"Mum I'm fine!" I knew it sounded rude but right now I needed to fix things with Harrison. Mum would forgive me.

My phone screen was blank. There were no messages; none from Lottie, none from Kieran or Nate and worst of all, none from Harrison. Had I really lost him? What had Lottie been saying to him? All these thoughts ran through my head and I couldn't help but start to cry. Harrison was my best friend, even more so than Lottie, and I needed him. I didn't care who saw the tears this time; instead I let them fall without any effort to clear them. Senna and Mum were passing me tissues and asking questions, neither of which I took or answered. Everything was a blur. I knew I needed to get a grip and deep down I knew that Harrison would never really be gone. We'd shared too much. I couldn't help but question my reaction to his silence. Did I love him back? Or was I just scared to be without him? Either way I knew I needed to find the answer. I'd been hurting him for too long now.

I was aware that Mum and Senna had left, I just couldn't find the words to ask where. When the room was completely empty from any nurses, I wiped the last few remaining tears from my eyes and turned my attention back to my phone. Scrolling through my previous messages I stopped on Harrison's name. Opening the feed, I couldn't help but smile at his last message. He always had a way of using as many emoticons as possible, whether they be random food icons, the peach being his favourite, or smiley faces. Each message carried so much thought and love it was hard not to reply to them. We'd often stay up all night talking even though we would have seen each other all day. I'd always thought our relationship was unbreakable and right now I wished I was right. I started typing: *Harrison, I'm so sorry.* I paused wondering whether I should carry on. Was it wise to pour my heart out when I didn't really understand my emotions myself? All I could do was long for a happy ending; trust faith that what shall be will be. I carried on:

Lottie told me everything. You're my everything and without you I don't know what I'll do. I wouldn't be Kass without you. You've been my strength through so much and I can't thank you enough. I know you want more than what I've ever given you and I'm so sorry I can't give it you. Please don't think it's because I don't love you because I do, more than anything. I've been so scared of losing you, I've probably rested too much on you, relied on you too much. I know you'll probably say you don't mind but that's because you're a better person than I'll ever be. I've been selfish Harrison and you deserve better. Please don't say your silence is because you're done with our friendship. I understand if it is and if it is the case then promise me one think, you'll be happy? Your Kass, x.

I re-read the message repeatedly, wondering whether it was too much. I'd given him the wrong impression for too long and it was the last thing I wanted to do. I needed to be honest with him but everything I wrote seemed to be selfish; asking him to put my feelings before his and just accept our friendship for what it was. I needed him to be my best friend but I couldn't commit to anything more, not fully. With Adam still being present and Senna lurking around I was in no position to give Harrison what he deserved. My finger hovered over the send button as I read the message one last time. Making the first move was new territory for me but one that clearly had to be done. Touching down on the screen, there was no going back now. I would either be searching for a Harrison replacement, a task that seemed impossible, or I'd be so thankful for having another chance. Either way I couldn't help but think that Lottie was responsible for all of this. I hadn't even fallen out with Harrison but his silence appeared the result of her meddling.

After staring at my phone for a few minutes I decided to plug myself in. Torturing myself wasn't going to get me out of this place. I looked around the room; other patients all being seen to by doctors. I was a fraud in here; I wasn't ill, just heartbroken at the thought of losing my best friend. Apple music was on shuffle, playing all these songs I'd never heard of. I was quick to skip any tragic love song in the hope to avoid any more crying but the distraction was fully welcomed nonetheless. Focusing my mind on each new lyric, to pass some time, soon turned into a kind of sad, guessing game. Being in hospital really was very boring. It was then that company arrived. First I saw Mum, then Senna and then hiding at the back was Harrison. His usually bright eyes appeared sad and distant, and his beaming smile was far from present. Stepping out from behind Senna, I could see he was holding his mobile. Had he seen my message? Was that why he was here? Mum came over and took the headphones out of my ears;

"Darling do you not want to say something?" I looked from him to her then back to him.

"Hi…" I hoped for his response to be a bit longer but, clearly feeling awkward he replied with the same. Luckily Mum was there, "you two need to sort this out. I am not going through this again Kass. You don't belong in a place like this. Come on Senna let's go." I don't think Senna had a choice. Why he was still hanging around was a question for another time.

Harrison took a seat next to my bed, thankfully he spoke first.

"Kass I've been so worried but Lottie said you didn't want to see me." The anger boiled over me, "I knew that cow had been stirring. I knew our friendship meant too much to you."

"That's why I'm here Kass, what's this message all about? I don't understand it." He shoved the message in front of my eyes as if I hadn't seen it before. I didn't have it in me to explain I'd read the message on numerous occasions; instead I tried to explain.

"Lottie said I was selfish. Oh Harrison, she said that I'd been a shit friend to you, that you deserved better because of how you felt."

"Kass she has no idea how I feel. I thought we'd spoken about this before? You're my best friend and always will be but we can't be anything more. I can't really imagine it being anything more, it would be like kissing my sister." I couldn't help but let out a huge sigh of relief. His smile gave me the reassurance I needed; he meant it, and from that moment I truly believed we were on the same page. A huge weight had been lifted off my shoulders, leaving only the saga with Adam and Senna to occupy them. With that he came and joined me on my bed and gave me one of his huge bear hugs. I'd missed him so much.

My day had instantly turned from rubbish to fun. Harrison had brought his usual witty banter and had me laughing for the remainder of the visiting hours. By the end of them, he'd informed me of all Kieran's latest girl fails. I'd only been in here just over a week yet there were several stories I'd missed out on. We'd rearranged our shopping trip and planned all these other adventures, just me and him. It sounded perfect and made me more determined to get out of this place quickly. Saying goodbye to him was surprisingly easy as I knew it wasn't forever. Harrison had promised to come back in tomorrow, saying "I'll bring the peaches." His humour was automatic. I laughed and hugged him goodbye.

Harrison's visit certainly changed my mood, unfortunately I still found myself in hospital. These four walls were enough to make even the sanest of people feel depressed; still it gave me time to think. I often liked to think, little good it did though. Now I'd had the reassurance Harrison and I were on the same page, my thoughts drifted to Tattoo Man. Why had he really visited me everyday? It wasn't as if his visits were just to accompany his Mum. No; Maggie had warned me to stay away and I had been but it was evident that Senna had not been given the same lecture. Yet again he could have chosen to ignore it. He really had just wanted to see me; check that I was ok. My mind was heading for a disappointment as I could feel my hopes building up and there was nothing I could do about it. My thoughts went from Senna to Adam then back again. Did the fact he was related to one of the worst ex's out there, stop me from being happy again?

I was still drugged up, so much so I soon found myself slipping to sleep again. My dreams were happier than they were yesterday, still I had a lot of decisions to make. I could feel and smell the ocean, the Mexican waves crashing against my bare feet. The sun was beaming against my face and for once all the struggles seemed to disappear. I felt happy, the happiest I'd been since that Friday back in May. The dream would soon be over but the honesty of it would hopefully be relived next month when I was on true Mexico soil. I didn't know how the next few weeks were going to plan out but one thing was for sure; I couldn't embarrass myself or anyone else again. There was to be no more wine throwing, no more throwing punches and no more public crying. University would soon be upon me and I don't think that kind of behaviour would be appropriate.

It was the following morning when I awoke and for a moment I forgot where I was. The sun was shining through the grotty pale yellow curtains and the old lady in the bed in the corner was already moaning about the ward's noise. It had to make you smile; it was the only entertainment you would get in this place. I couldn't help but fixate on the poor nurse's attempt to calm the lady down. If anything, she was the one making the noise. The smile must have stuck on my face. "What's made you so happy this morning?" It was Senna.

"Senna what are you doing here?" I never thought I'd feel it but for the first time since our reintroduction in May, I really didn't want to see him. Had his Mum's words finally started to sink in? And for a moment I was back in my garden, *'I really need you to stay away from Adam and my son."* Maggie's words were so powerful that relaying them in my head made me even more determined to get Adam and Tattoo Man out of my life. His visits the past week had meant nothing, had they? "That's a lovely way to greet someone Kass. I brought you breakfast," and with that he handed over a fresh, warm croissant. They smelled divine, it was just a shame I wasn't a fan of them; still the thought was nice. Then again it really did show how little we knew about each other. He was an acquaintance and nothing more. Maggie was the friend, not Senna and certainly not Adam. Shaking my head to refrain from my changing my mind I handed them back. "No Senna I mean why are you here? Why have you been here all week?" His face looked hurt.

"Kass I needed to make sure you were ok. I've been an idiot. You're a special girl you know, I just can't hurt you like my cousin did." I needed him to stop talking before the next bit came but it was too late. "I like you Kass, you just deserve better. I'm sorry if I've led you on I just really wanted to be friends." There it was, the exact words Adam had said every time he had decided to leave. Friends? What did that even mean? I had my friends and they were more than enough.

I wanted to tell him he hadn't hurt me, tell him I didn't care and that friends were fine but it would all be a lie. Senna Jackson really hadn't done anything, he just had the same charm and excuses Adam used. So, yes, Mum was right I probably did deserve better but that wasn't Senna, Adam's or anyone else's decision to make. I couldn't help but go back to the time we were all at my house. Everything seemed so easy back then and Adam really didn't seem an issue. The way in which Senna had stuck up for me that night, I thought showed he cared and more about me than his cousin. It was silly really; of course he would always be on Adam's side, they were related and I was merely just the daughter of his Mother's best friend. I needed Senna to disappear and quickly.

"Senna look I don't care, please go. Your mother was right." Shit, ok I really didn't want to put Maggie in it but right now I needed all the help I could get. I was in a pretty vulnerable place with no one around to get rid of this unwanted visitor.
"What do you mean my mother?" Well I knew that response was coming but I'd said enough so I just rolled over in hope that he would get the message and just leave.

After a few minutes, I heard the rustling of the brown paper bag, that contained the croissants, being put down on my bedside table and then footsteps leaving. He was finally gone. I wasn't going to cry or get upset but instead reached for my phone to find Maggie's number. She deserved a heads up. Whilst it rang I gave the ward a once over; the old woman in the corner now had a visitor who I assume was her son, the man in the bed next to me also had a visitor and the two patients opposite me were deep in conversation, leaving just me and I was, well, alone. For once it felt good. I felt back in control, knowing that every emotion I felt right now was truly justified and right. I could feel sad about what could have been but I knew in this instance trusting my head was the right thing to do. Just like throughout my whole schooling career my head had got me through, not my heart.

On the other end of the phone it was still ringing and just as I was about to hang up a breathless Maggie picked up. I didn't want to ask what she was up to; it could have been one of two things I was just hoping that I hadn't interrupted something important. "Hey Kass, how are you doing?" I really wanted to ignore that question as I felt I needed to convince myself for a tad longer that I was ok before saying it out loud. Maggie was like my mum; they could read my tone of voice down to a T and would know instantly if I was fibbing. "Maggie, I just wanted to give you the heads up. I think I may have put you in it with Senna. I'm really sorry I didn't mean to, he just wouldn't leave."

"Kass calm down, I really don't care what you've told him. I'll tell him to his face if I have to. He needs to leave you alone. If anything, I should be sorry. I should have told him to stay away from you especially when you're so weak. When is your Mum bringing you home?"
"I didn't know she was?"
"Oh, she told me that you were coming home today."
She sounded confused but I really hoped she was right. This place was giving me the creeps and surely wasn't the ideal place for someone that struggled with emotions. I wouldn't say it was a particularly sick ward, with no one really seeming on death's door but it was hardly lively nonetheless.

"I really hope so Maggie."
"I know darling, we all want you home. I know your sister has missed you." Not as much as I'd missed her. Malia and I were as close as an eighteen and thirteen-year-old could be. Mum would tell me she looked up to me and in a way, I really hope she did. I just hated that she had to witness my romantic failures before even getting to experience love herself. If it was the last thing I did I had to convince her that not all guys were bad. Maybe I could just joke that I left the good ones for her. "I've missed her too Mags." A nurse was hovering at the end of my bed. "Anyway, I think I've got to go so I'll see you soon."

"Ok Kass, you take care and I'll see you when you're home. Just Bob and I," and with that she hung up. Just her and Bob sounded perfect. Bob would bring his witty banter and hopefully they'd be one of those steak chops waiting for me. It was true what they said; hospital food really was crap. The nurse was now looking at my charts. When she finished, she put them back in the slot at the end of my bed before turning to walk away. I found myself asking before even thinking; "Sorry, when can I go home?"

The young nurse turned around and smiled, "Today, your Mum will be here soon."

Egyptian Cotton

Being home was better than expected. My own bed seemed ten times bigger and the Egyptian cotton sheets were worlds apart from the thin, bobbly ones I'd been used to the week before. Normality wasn't as far away as it was a few weeks ago. A smile was plastered on my face as I snuggled into my duvet. Yes, it was only eight o'clock but it had been an exhausting day. I arrived home from hospital to a driveway party; Maggie and Bob were amongst the guests and just as she'd promised there was no Adam and no Senna. It was a relief, yet upsetting at the same time. Senna clearly cared but for once I honestly believed Adam was right; I did deserve better. From first impressions Senna was nowhere near Adam on the waste-of-space scale however I refused to stay around long enough to find out. My heart had been through enough and now it needed protecting.

As usual, Maggie had welcomed me with a beaming smile and a second-best hug to a Mum's one. There was nothing quite like it; my extended family were all I needed and no man, even prince charming, would compare to their love. Maggie's embrace was heaven but there was only one real person I wanted to see; my Mal. She may have been my younger sister, six years younger to be precise, but the bond we had was indescribable, even if it was a little one sided. Still, I took no offence. She was an innocent girl and probably didn't realise just how proud she made me.

Malia was nowhere to be seen. She wasn't glued to her phone, like usual, wasn't in the garden and wasn't in her bedroom. Instead I found her in the last place I looked, the place where usually I'd be annoyed; my room. She sat crossed legged on my bed holding my photo frame. The frame held one of my favourite images of her and I; the one I used as my phone and iMac screensaver. Mal must have been a few months old and was slumped over my lap. No matter what mood I was in it never failed to make me smile and recently was looked at more and more for that main purpose. When she saw me she jumped up, probably expecting the backlash she normally received when I found her in my room. Instead I just pulled her in for a hug.

"Mal are you ok?" She remained silent but nodded against my chest and hugged me a little tighter. "Oh, Mal it's ok. I'm ok." I felt like she needed the reassurance but honestly, I was taken back as to her reaction. Malia was always the one to not show emotion. She hated the attention apparently whereas I needed comfort, a sign to show how I was feeling was normal. That was the thing with Mal and I, we were so similar over certain things yet worlds apart when it came to emotionally driven acts. I was hoping it was just her age and that she wasn't always going to come across as a hard person. Even though it hadn't brought any happiness to me, I needed her to understand love wasn't all that bad.

It was hard to know what to say. I'd never seen Malia like this before. Was she generally worried about me? We stayed in the hug for several moments before she let her grip slide.

"Kass, please don't be ill again." Her response came as a huge shock; I wouldn't say I was ill, I just handled heart upset in an abnormal way to other people. Ill was people really suffering, often people that would leave heartbroken family members behind. I was just a teenage girl who would leave no one and would die of heartbreak rather than anything else. Well that's what I thought but standing here now I realised I wasn't alone; Malia needed me in more ways than I ever knew. She was a perfect little sister, even if a little odd at times.

"Mal, I'm not ill. I'm here. Anyway what were you doing in here? There's a party out there." The mood needing changing and quickly. The way my heart was acting recently, I was unsure as to how much morbid conversation it could handle. I stepped away so that Malia's face was no longer hidden. I could tell she'd been crying but decided on not to pry. She glanced a smile my way as her way of pretending everything was ok and then we left. Closing my bedroom door behind us, I watched Malia slump off downstairs. I couldn't help myself but pause and watch. Without meaning too she'd given me reason to hope. I couldn't and wouldn't upset her again. I knew what I needed to do, just not now and not tonight, and with that I followed Malia downstairs.

The driveway was decked with a table and chairs rather than the usual cars; us Green's didn't do normality. Maggie and Bob were deep in conversation with Mum and Dad. Malia had found conversation with one of her friends and I, well I just stood there taking everything in. Everyone here cared; in return the overwhelming feeling my heart felt was one of love and support. I'd only been in hospital just over a week but that seemed enough to make more than my family worry. It was strange really, the reason I was in hospital was nowhere to be seen. There was no Lottie, no Senna and no Adam. Harrison had text me to say he was running late, and Kieran and Nate were standing over the food as per usual. Now I knew Malia was ok it was time to mingle.

Kieran was the first to see me. "Kass you drama queen!" His sarcasm was playful even though justified. Seriously though, who gets rushed to hospital with a broken heart? He still pulled me in to one of his bear hugs, for Nate to only join in. I was in the middle of a guy sandwich and funnily enough it felt normal. I felt as chilled as I had been since Tattoo Man entered my life. Along with my family, the Jacksons and my best friends, I didn't need anyone else.
"Oi guys, come on! Nate get me a burger. All I've eaten for the past week is shitty hospital food!"

To be honest it really wasn't that bad, I'd just missed my Mum's homemade cooking and my Dad's top-notch BBQ's. I needed the awkward hug to end and my stomach to stop rumbling. Everyone was talking, eating and drinking. The afternoon turned to evening and people went from completely sober to slightly tipsy. This was what summer afternoon's were made for; fun, friends and laughter. I just hoped the next time was for a reason other than a hospital discharge. Harrison had come and gone, bringing the biggest and most beautiful bouquet of flowers. He'd promised to come back tomorrow for a bigger and better catch up but vowed that his bed was calling. It had only turned seven so I doubted it highly but couldn't find the energy to question it.

The party, if you could call it that, carried on way into the night. By quarter to eight I was struggling to keep my eyes open, the hospital routine still firmly drilled into me. After doing my rounds of goodbyes I left the mob to carry on drinking. Normally I would have hated leaving so early but this time I was rather content; I would have only ruined the mood and Mum seemed to be smiling again. She had offered to send people home but it was evident that she needed the fun just as much as I needed my bed.

"Kass it's so good to have you home," she'd said before I headed off upstairs. People had been acting as if I'd been away for months, still the love was deeply felt. It was then that it hit; my panic attack had effected more people than just myself.

That was the thing with having such a close family.

Every emotion felt was spread amongst everyone. If you were down, everyone knew about it. My family, Maggie and Bob deserved some happiness and I was planning to do everything I could to change our luck. A full detox was in order, starting with clearing any negative people and thoughts from my life. I was tempted to sort things out with Lottie but I was still so angry. She'd purposefully set out to drive a wedge between myself and Harrison, and I still couldn't understand why. Was she jealous? Or did she simply think she was right? I wanted to believe the latter, hoping that my judgement couldn't have been that wrong. Picking up my phone, I was just about to send her a message until I was interrupted by a knock on my door. It was Maggie. "Kass, it's Mags. Can I come in?"

I reached for the door handle to see her standing in the doorway with an envelope in her hand. "Hey, Mags. What's up?" By this time I'd wiped my minimal makeup off and was dressed into my night slip. Maggie had seen me in worst states so I wasn't that concerned.

"Darling how are you feeling?" Before I could answer she'd carried on; "I didn't bring Senna like I promised but he asked me to give you this." And with that she handed me the envelope. "You don't need to read it. I think he thinks you'll end up throwing it away but he asked me to give it you anyway." Her voice was hoarse as she said it. I took the envelope of her and became fixated on the neat name written on the front, 'Kassia, x.' He'd used my name rather than my nickname; something that make whatever was written inside more real, written from the heart. I debated tearing it in half; Senna had already caused a big enough impact on my life. It was strange to think that I'd known him my entire life. Our naked paddling pool days safely behind us and significantly unimaginable. Our story, Senna's and mine, was one of two halves; there was the one of young and innocent childhood where we were pushed together through our mother's friendship, then there was the one now; one of confused feelings. The gap in between was simply that. I had no recollection of what had happened to him and to why he'd disappeared. Apparently, it was a story Maggie never wanted to tell, one which clearly brought back bad memories. The fact that he had been sent off to boarding school should have sent the alarm bells going; this guy was trouble but instead of stepping back, I jumped forward with both feet.

I eventually got around to replying, "Thanks Maggie." It was a pretty lame response even for me but I wasn't entirely sure as what to say. Was I going to read it or was it going straight in the bin? My mind hadn't been made up. Since the other day, when I demanded Senna to go, he hadn't even crossed my mind. It was typical though, especially in my life; just as you thought you had it sorted, something would come play with your mind. Senna was a disaster waiting to happen. In the perfect world, we'd be fine as just friends, mainly for the sake of Mum and Maggie. Instead he insisted on making things impossible. I'd been warned off him by his Mother of all people and she was surely someone that knew him better than me. I knew nothing about him and shallowly, had only been attracted to him by his smile and charming

Chat.

Putting the envelope to one side, I turned to Maggie. I had to ask; "Maggie can I ask you something?"

"Anything Kass"

"Why did you really warn me off Senna?" I think I knew the answer but I needed to hear it.

"Kass, I'm sorry I did that. It really wasn't my place but after seeing you upset the other day I needed to protect you. My boy is a hard one to figure out. It's easy to know when he likes someone but I just think he gets scared easily." She sighed before carrying on, "He's scared of commitment, of being hurt again but you can blame his cousin for that." My face clearly showed confusion, "Kass he's not a bad lad and doesn't intentionally hurt girls but what his cousin did was wrong. I'm honestly surprised they are still as close as they are."

"Mags, I'm lost."

"Oh, did he not tell you?"

"Tell me what?"

"Senna found his last real girlfriend in bed with Adam. He blames himself really. He was addicted to his job and gave her hardly any attention. Still, I could never blame him. Adam betrayed him in the worst way possible."

I was dumbfounded; I knew Adam was an idiot but I never had him down as a person who could do that. It was from that one revelation that I realised I'd got the whole situation wrong. Senna couldn't be compared to Adam, couldn't be tarred with the same brush. Adam was a coward, Senna was simply scared of being hurt again.

"Kass, I wanted to thank you though. That night you guys met again…" My mind flashed back to the night at The Baggers. "Well he came back with a smile on his face. A real one. One that his father and I hadn't seen for a long time. I knew there must have been a girl, I just didn't realise it would be you. You're a special girl Kass. I see you and your sister as part of my own family and if my boy hadn't gone through what he had then I know he'd treat you right."

"Maggie, it's ok. Thank you for telling me. You can tell Senna, I'll read it," and I meant it. I needed to know what he'd wrote. Not as a way of knowing what to do next, but as a way of knowing how he felt. There was no guarantee that whatever was inside would give me any answers but it was a start.

I hugged Maggie goodbye. "You get some sleep and if you ever want to talk, just message me."

"Thanks Mags," and with that she left. I was thankful for her visit but it had left my head with a whirlwind of questions. Why would Adam do that? When did he do it? Before, after or during our on-off relationship? It wasn't Senna I needed answers from, it was Adam. I climbed out of bed to grab my laptop. Opening a new email I started typing. I didn't really know what I was writing but I just let my fingers take full control on my keypad. My mind was full of so much anger towards this man it was only fair I shared it.

'Adam.

I probably shouldn't be writing to you as it will open up a form of communication I've tried to avoid ever since last summer. Truth is, as I'm sure you're aware I've been in hospital and no this wasn't your fault but it's not healthy for me to keep anger and heartache bottled up. Why should you carry on with your life when you are still ruining mine? You hurt me. I was a naïve seventeen-year-old girl who didn't know what love was but thank you for ruining my first experience of it. You jumped in and out of my life whenever you felt like it and I let you. You knew you could get away with anything. I forgave you more times than I should have, something you evidently thrived off. I would say I'm the stupid one for not learning after the first time but truth is you're the stupid one. I'm not the undeserving, unworthy girl you made me out to be. I was not obsessed with you but in fact saw the best in you when no one else did.

I want you to know that I no longer love you but instead pity you. You carry on hurting girls, sleeping around as it's quite clear that you will never learn. One of these days you'll wake up and feel truly alone.

Oh and Adam, what you did to Senna was the biggest betrayal of all. Don't worry I'll make him see the true person you really are.

I don't need a reply.

Kassia.'

The full stop should emphasize the no reply comment. Reading back over my message once more, I was happy with it. It wasn't brutal, but if anything quite mature. Adam had to stop ruining lives before he ran out of people that would be there for him. It felt abnormal writing such a harsh email to him as I'd always been so nice, so understanding but after unravelling more of Adam's painful deceit I felt it was only right. A part of me would always love him, I just could never let him know. He was my first love, the one that angled your life and taught you the do's and don'ts about relationships. Sitting here now, I struggled to come up with anything good that had come out of Adam and me. He let me know what love was but it was far from the fairy-tale stories I had dreamt of.

Before pressing send I let out a huge sigh of relief. Was I even doing the right thing? I knew Adam wouldn't just accept my message without replying; it just wasn't in his makeup. He hated backlash, hated people slagging him off but this one was surely well-deserved. Not only had he ruined my life for over a year but had ruined any potential relationship between his cousin and me. It's not as if that's what I expected as I didn't really know Senna well enough. All I did know was that those spoken about butterflies were present. Senna gave me a sense of hope and excited me in ways Adam never did.

It was sent. Adam would be receiving the first direct message from myself in almost a year. I hated Adam in the same way I loved him, whole-heartedly.

Part of me knew that Adam was always going to be part of my life; the same part wanted it to happen. Adam was cute; blonde, blue-eyed and charming. On the outside, he was picture-frame perfect, the kind of guy that every Mother would want their child to be with and let's be honest he'd make excellent offspring. For me, my experience with Adam was torture. I worshiped the ground he walked on when we were together but suffered horrendous heartache every time he called time on our romance. He saw my love as nothing but a game, something he could take and push away whenever he pleased. It was after around the tenth time I knew my love was not reciprocated. His efforts of making me believe he cared were only attempts and certainly didn't stick.

The message was hopefully one of closure. I didn't need Adam. Senna didn't need Adam. He was better off left in the past. Closing my laptop, I placed it on the floor and turned my attention to the envelope that laid beside me. Did I really want to read it? Surely it was just better to put both Adam and Senna in my black box and not take them out again. The summer ahead should be one of joy and memories not tears and heartbreak. Still, the temptation was too strong and with that I found myself tearing open the envelope. I snuggled deeper into my bedsheets and created a fort around me. Cooky was on one side and my mountain of cushions on the other. The letter was written in red pen and the writing was surprisingly neat for a man.

'Kass,

I'd put out my hand for a handshake if I could. I know that's when you're most comfortable. Before I start, you need to know I'm pretty shit at writing and emotions. My head and heart never seem to be on the same page. I guess I can blame Adam for that but that's a story for another time..."

Something told me I already knew that story.

I know you told me to leave you alone but I had to get something off my chest. When I saw you in The Baggers I had no clue who you were, no clue that I'd already seen you naked on numerous occasions. Trust me I wish I remembered. But it wasn't your looks that attracted me to you; it was your eyes. Your eyes carry so much light and happiness Kass, they truly are special. You have no idea how amazing you are. Your smile can light up the room but your confidence is all inverted. I knew you were funny from the first time you held out you hand as a welcome gesture. It was a first Kass. I'm used to girls loving my attention but with you, you didn't seem that interested. I was like a cold glass of water, you could drink it or leave it. The way you made me feel was all new; I needed to know why you were different. Why didn't you act like every other girl had? If I was being honest, it was a turn on in its own entity. You were different…mysterious.

What a cocky sod. What made him think he was God's gift?

You told me to leave you alone and I will but I need you to know I have never meant to mess you around. Mum sees you as her daughter and I will listen to her. You do deserve better. I'm shit with girls and even worse when it comes to relationships. We don't really know each other but at the same time I haven't felt this close to a girl ever since my ex. When I saw you crying that night on your bed I knew I wanted to stop your tears; to be the guy that restored your faith in men. I'm sorry I failed. Mum's right, I really am cut from the same cloth as Adam. I don't know where this is going or what the purpose of this letter is but I guess all I'm trying to say is that I have never pretended with you. I care, I'm just shocking when it comes to replying to people. Next time you want to chuck something at me, why not try the water? It's free and wont sting as much when it gets me in the eye, unless that was your aim. Which if so, good aim! Not just a pretty girl eh? On a more serious note, the connection you clearly feel between us is real as I feel it too.

You know where I am.

Senna Jackson x'

Why he signed it off with his full name I'd never know. His words hurt but carried so much emotion it was hard not to believe them. I was thankful that I wasn't the only one that felt it; that felt the connection. However, I was left even more confused; Senna's words had been similar to the ones Adam had once said to me, the only difference being I actually believed them this time. There was something about the whole situation, how Maggie had warned him away, how I knew about his ex-girlfriend and how he'd been so open. For someone who lacked in relationships, he certainly made up for it in words. What girl wouldn't fall for someone that not only looked good, but had the smile to die for and the words of a romantic god?

I re-read the letter half a dozen times before folding it back up and placing it back in its envelope. My eyes were now severely struggling to stay open, so much so even matchsticks would suffer. The words of the letters stayed wedged in my mind, one sentence in particular being more prominent than others, '*the connection you clearly feel between us is real as I feel it too.*' I don't know where he got that idea from. I'd never told him that he'd instantly played havoc with my heart; he clearly just had a bigger ego than I first thought. I knew he was confident from the first time I saw him in The Baggers, but even I was taken back from just how much. Still, there were a few of his words that made me smile; why the hell did I waste the wine!?

My back hit my bed hard, my mattress being ten times harder than the thin hospital one I'd been used to. I tried to switch my brain off with little success. After lying there for what seemed like a good hour, I went to plan B. Grabbing my laptop I found my yoga playlist in the hope that my inner zen would resurface and that sleep would easily follow. I tried to focus on the whale music, focusing on our up and coming holiday. If there was one thing I needed it was a holiday. The Mexican breeze and sun would never see such appreciation.

Eventually, slowly but surely, I felt myself drifting off. The sun was starting to die out and my curtains provided a solid shut out to its last rays. There was no hospital shuffling, no abnormally loud snoring and no moaning patients; instead just pure calmness, something that was not just welcomed but embraced. With the help of my whales, my eyes were soon shut and my mind had wondered far from the stresses of reality. I dreamt of Mexico that night; sun, sea and, well, not that. In fact, the whole dream only consisted of my family, the ones I could always rely on. Mum and I were going through the cocktail list from top to tale in typical Green fashion. Dad was partaking in the odd Mojito and Mal was glued to her phone. Everything was as it should be and I could whole-heartedly say I was happy.

The following morning I was woken by the sound of banging in the kitchen. I'd fallen asleep in the most awkward position and my arms and side were certainly paying the price now. My ears were still being serenaded by whale music, meaning the sound from downstairs must have been pretty loud. It can't have been that loud; I'd gone to bed so early I expected it to be before eight. I loved my bed but a solid twelve hours was even enough for me. Reaching for my phone, I was shocked to see that it was pushing on eleven. Had I really slept for that long? And why had no one woken me? I would have normally be getting the 'you lazy sod' treatment by now. Wiggling out of my crimpled position I rolled over the envelope, the envelope I'd tried so hard to forget about. Now daylight had hit again, it was time to face the truth.

Senna's letter was real and the words on the page were in pen. They couldn't be rubbed out and couldn't be taken back.

Part of me wanted to reply, the other part of me wanted to forget. If there was one thing that cut deeper than Senna's words it was his mother's. I'd never seen her that timid before as to when she handed me the envelope. It was clear that even she was fearful as to what it contained. That was the thing with Maggie, she barely wore her heart on her sleeve but when she did, everyone could feel it. The air suddenly had a chill and the hairs on my arms stood tall. Senna was scarring my heart deeper than I wanted him to and for the first time since meeting him I was scared. I wasn't scared of him, just the hold he was getting over me. It was another Adam situation all over again but I was an adult now and learning from my mistakes was surely something that came with the higher status.

After wrapping my dressing gown around me I reached for the envelope I had left on my bed. Without even thinking my fist grasped around it, scrunching it into an unreadable ball. Whether it was an instinctive action or not, it was one clearly fuelled by anger. The emotions that boiled inside of me, though, were aimed at myself and not Senna. How could I let a few simple words get to me? I was the one that was good with words; I should know a lie when I read it. Senna couldn't mean a word he wrote, he was related to Adam and lies came naturally to him. In his own words, they were made from the same cloth.

Closing my eyes, I knew what I had to do. Throwing the ball of lies against my bedroom wall, I found myself falling into a heap against my bedframe. I knew all this sadness and anger was no good for my heart or health but I couldn't help myself. In ways, Senna had affected me more ways than Adam ever did. Even deep soul searching wasn't going to give me the answers I needed. What was it about this arrogant sod that was so magnetising? Was I really that much of a sucker for a smile? Or was it because I still needed a connection to Adam? Maybe that was it, maybe I was still in love with Adam. Maybe the feelings I tried so hard to push to the back of my heart had resurfaced. All I did know was that my heart was well and truly beating.

I'll think about you

Downstairs Mum and Dad were clearing up the remains of last night. Wine bottles and beer cans littered our patio and the coal remains of a successful BBQ remained in the pit. They seemed to be in high spirits, both singing along to Smooth Radio. It couldn't help but make you smile and in that one instant the fears of my near panic attack relapse vanished. No one needed to know about my almost breakdown. I needed to get on top of this, needed to stop being controlled by feelings that were unwanted.

"You guys seem happy."
"Hey darling, how are you feeling?" Mum came trotting over, giving me a hug before I could even answer. After that came an orange juice and fruit bowl being pushed in my face. My Mother's subtle hint for me to eat was laughable. You had to love her.

"Thanks Mum, I'm just glad to be home." That wasn't a lie. Hospital had made me appreciate the small things that I'd taken for granted. I took my glass and bowl outside and perched on a seat facing the rising sun. The fresh air was heaven. You didn't get this in hospital. It wasn't long before everyone joined me, including Malia. It was enough to make your heart burst with love. With the four of us being miles away from the rest of our family it was good that we were as close as we were. Don't get me wrong, we had our ups and downs but with a joker of a Dad it was hard not to smile at twice a day. Then we had Mum, the one that had our back no matter what. It was hard not to feel safe and loved with her around. Then there was Malia, my little me. She was as perfect as little sisters go, even if a bit annoying at times.

The conversation went from last night to tonight. I was very much out of the loop, not having a clue what they were on about. My mind went into its own little world not even trying to get on board and contribute. I could see mouths moving but couldn't hear the words coming out. Even Malia was talking so it must have been about something interesting but even that wasn't enough to snap me out of my muse. I let the three of them chat, nod and laugh for a while. My heart felt warm seeing them happy. I knew they had struggled to find a lot of joy lately mainly because of me. The guilt I carried was heavy but it was going to change. If I deserved better than Adam and Senna then they deserved a happy daughter and sister.

"Kass what do you think? You think you'll be up for it?" I stared blankly at Mum, hoping that she'd give a bit more detail about the thing I was meant to be up for. She just looked back, giving me the once over before repeating herself. Still I had no reply.
"Sorry Mum, what?"
"Have you been listening to a word we've said?" I couldn't find the balls to admit I'd in fact zoned out as soon as they'd mentioned tonight, instead I just shook my head.

"Some things never change with you do they?" She laughed but I knew under normal circumstances it would have annoyed her and probably would have started the whole 'you get it from your father' malarkey. He was prone to not hearing things first time even though I was sure he just had selective hearing; something that came with the territory of living with three girls.

Mum went on to explain how she had the whole day planned starting with the 'perfect' day with her girls; this always consisted of shopping and cocktails, or mocktails for Mal. I was still feeling a little weak but even I couldn't turn down the chance to actually doing something. It was the evening activity that made me apprehensive.

"Kass I know you love this place and I don't want you being embarrassed of going back there. We thought a family meal at The Swallow could be just what you need. There's a steak waiting for you and I've even put in a special order with Senna in advanced. Sweetheart, don't worry Adam's not working tonight."

I didn't have it in me to say it wasn't Adam I wanted to avoid. Senna's screwed up letter flashed back and just like that the sun was covered by a big black cloud. It was a sign, it just had to be. Tattoo Man was already surrounding me, little signs letting me know he was more dangerous than first thought.

My faced must have said it all. I was not only surprised that Mum had spoken to Senna, especially after the way she acted around him at my hospital bedside, but also that she thought I'd want to go back there. After the last time The Swallow had gone from my favourite to worst place in the space of a few hours. Then there was the ordeal of Harry's fist and Senna's face. How could I possibly show my face again?

I didn't know they would come; I thought I was stronger. The tears starting rolling from my ears before I could excuse myself. I didn't want the questions, and had had enough of the attention and pity. The air suddenly seemed stuffy and unbreathable and I could feel another panic attack coming on. I don't know what had come over me. Mum was soon straddling me, telling me everything was going to be ok. I had little faith in it right now but I needed to hear it nonetheless. There was no way I was going back to hospital so I had to pull myself together if it was the last thing I did.

"Kass, look at me." Mum's t-shirt had a tear-stained patch where my head had taken great comfort in her arms. Her eyes showed fear and worry. I hated seeing her like this. Why couldn't I just be the perfect daughter? One with no worries, no problems and one that could honestly say they were happy, or if not that at least content.

"Kass, I thought you were feeling better. If it's too much we don't need to go later. I…"she looked over to Dad for a sign of encouragement. "We, just thought it would be nice. We want you to know we're here Kass. I even invited Harry." The sound of his name made me instantly smile. If there was such thing of the right medicine for my mental state it was him.

"Mum, I'm sorry"
"Darling you don't need to be sorry"
"I do, I make you unhappy. Why can't someone just love me properly? I've never felt so alone."
The words came out of my mouth before I could stop them and with that the tears fell hard again. They were different tears to last time though. I wasn't about to collapse, I wasn't even about to fall apart. If anything, I felt relived. The tears were a sign of letting go. Both Senna and Adam weren't worth it, they weren't worth my tears and they certainly weren't worth my love.
"Oh Kass, someone does love you. There's someone out there for both my babies," and with that she pulled Malia into the hug. "But for now you'll just have to make do with mine and your Father's."

She was right; I knew she was. Without even getting to know him I knew Senna was bad news but I also knew I had to keep my distance; at least until my heart stitched itself up again. Maggie was a huge part of my life but even that would have to be put on the back burner. A complete detox was in order, of Senna, or Adam and any potential man. Trying to explain this to Mum was one of the hardest things I'd ever done. All she wanted was her children to be happy, to be loved and to have the relationship she had with my Father. To them love was simple, to me it was the outcome of a funeral; sad, tear-ridden and lonely.

Sun, sea and tragedy

The month had surprisingly flown by. I'd done the impossible and avoiding all confrontation with any of the Jackson family, Maggie included. It didn't stop her sending me the occasional message, ensuring me that she understood but that she was there if I needed her. Her concern as nice even though ignored. I didn't want to upset her but no contact needed to remain at no contact. Mum was as supportive as ever and did everything she could to keep me distracted. There was no boy small talk, no romantic comedies and no early morning chats with Maggie. I had ensured her, even begged her, to not let my needs ruin her friendship with her best friend. She promised me it wouldn't but I'd already started planning something for the two of them for when I was feeling better.

Packing was harder than expected. It was simple for Dad *(I would say men but as any other male, apart from the crew, were a no go we'll stick with Dad)*. All he needed was a dozen pair of boxers, a few t-shirts, few shorts and the odd bit of evening wear. For us women it was far harder. There was not only the struggle of what dresses to take but then came the shoes, the accessories, the bags and all the stuff us females rely on to look good. Being a woman was hard! It was made even harder with the 23kg bag limit but after swapping a few shoes around and taking my fifth clutch bag out, I was finally ready. A week today I'd be on that plane. What could possibly go wrong between now and then?

That's when it happened. The one thing I, or anyone else, least expected. My phone had been almost forgotten about the past month, with me only checking it once a day. Harry, Kieran and Nate would phone the household or knock on the door if they needed me and, well, the Jackson's weren't the only people I were trying to avoid. Lottie and I hadn't spoken since my hospital visit and funnily enough I didn't miss it. I was no longer being over-ridden, over-spoken and finally had my boys back just the way I liked it. What made me check on this specific Tuesday, at precisely four in the afternoon, I'll never know.

The dreaded name Senna was plastered over my phone. There was something about it's unexpected presence that made it intriguing. I needed to know what he was saying but at the same time, knew it was dangerous territory. For the past four weeks he had respected the boundaries, given me the space I wanted and had accepted he was unworthy of my attention. This message was out of the blue in its simplest terms. What did he want? And why now? Unlocking my iPhone, nothing could have prepared me for the message that lied ahead.

'Kass, I know I'm the last person you want to hear from but I just thought you should know. I asked Mum to let me tell you. Adam was hit by a car last night and is in a coma. Call me. S x'

What was I meant to say to that? How was I meant to react? This was the guy I loathed for the past year, the guy that I wouldn't give the time of day for. Now he was possibly on death's door and I felt nothing but numbness. My holiday was ruined before I had even got on the plane. Next door I could hear Mum gasping on the phone to what I could assume was the tragic news. I slumped on my bed unable to group together my feelings, to even understand them. Was it shock? Was it sadness? Or was it joy? I prayed that it wasn't the latter; I hoped I had more heart than that.

Mum's phone conversation was far longer than I wanted it to be. Part of me wanted all the details, part of me wanted to stay in my happy world; the one I had done so well to remain in the past few weeks. I could here plenty of 'oh no's' and 'I'll tell her;' her clearly being me. Tell me what Mum? It was the waiting that made me realise I needed Adam to be ok. Not just for selfish reasons but for the Jackson's as a whole. The next few hours were a blur. Mum had finished her conversation almost in tears. The mood of the house had gone from excited to morbid in the matter of minutes and no one knew what to say. Mum and Dad were evidently worried as to how I would react but if anything my reaction was the most placid.

"Kass, I'll explain but I need you to promise me one thing? Promise me you won't bottle things up. If you need to talk I'm here."

"Promise Mum. Now how is he?" It came out as if I was generally concerned. Part of me was, the other part was convincing myself I should be. Mum explained everything even down to the goriest details. It had been the anniversary of Adam's Mum's death, the night where he should have been with his family rather than alone. Instead he had done the one thing that most men do in emotionally driven situations; drink. He had not only drank a little but had got so wasted that he found himself stumbling in front of cars.

"There was only so many cars he could avoid Kass before getting hit." Mum's voice was breaking as she said it. There was no hiding the fact that this was bad. Adam wasn't just hit, but instead mowed down. His alcohol levels hadn't helped and the impact to his brain was so severe that the doctor's couldn't get close enough to it to give a full examination. A coma was the only option.

Mum did her best to reassure me it was for the best; that Adam just needed time to heal. It sounded a lost cause even as she said it. I didn't call Senna like he asked. I didn't even reply to his message. Now wasn't the time to fake a friendship that I didn't want or need. Maggie had promised to keep us informed but insisted that our holiday wasn't ruined. Mum and Dad did their best to offer support to Maggie and Bob before we left but even they struggled to find the words. Adam wasn't dead but it didn't look good.

The night before we flew, things changed. It was three o'clock in the morning; the only light came from outside streetlights and the only noise came from the occasional car. That was until my phone started singing. "Senna what do you want?" There were mumbles at the other end of the phone then silence.

"Senna!"

"Kass, I need you. I need you here."

"Need me where?"

"I'm at the hospital."

I'm pretty sure visiting hours was well and truly gone, unless…

"Senna is Adam ok? He's still here?"

Then there were tears, not just sniffles, but actual tears. The man that was apparently so scared of emotions was showing them in the most heart-breaking way possible. I should have put the phone down, put my own feelings before his but there was something in his voice. He was broken, a feeling I only knew too well, and for some reason he wanted me.

"Senna it's ok, I'm on my way." The words escaped my mouth before I even had the chance to stop them. I was due at the airport in less than four hours for a holiday that I desperately needed but instead of being excited, I was back to being counsellor Kassia. If there was a career path I was destined to be it was clearly that.

Senna called me three times in the short time it took me to get dressed and drive eight miles up the road. I didn't care. It was from that night that I saw Senna differently. Under all those tattoos this man had a heart, not only a heart that could love but also one that was clearly breaking. We had no way of knowing how Adam would be but even I was praying he'd pull through. A part of me would always hold Adam in my heart; he'd been the reason for many scars but also for so much happiness. He'd let me know what love was, whether it was reciprocated or not. I could no longer blame him for hurting me but instead had to join Senna in hoping he would survive. Adam was simply better off alive.

He had so much love, not only through other people, but within himself. I didn't get to see much of it, but it was certainly there. Not that it mattered now, but I felt sorry for him. I'd been wrapped up in my own problems to remember the date that was lurching. A Mother's death was unimaginable, even on the easiest of days, but to be alone must have given it nothing but darkness.

Reaching the hospital, the night sky seemed to get a shade closer to noir. There were little stars in the sky and a sudden chill filled the air. Senna's figure was obvious; sitting directly under a street light, it was like something from a movie. The scene was set for some creepy shadow to appear. His body was crouched in the most unmanly way possible, the orange glow from the light making a perfect oval around him. As I edged my car closer to him, he didn't even flinch. His motionless body sent a shiver down my spine. If I didn't know how he was feeling from his phone call then I certainly did now.

I turned the engine off and just sat there, watching him. Under normal circumstances this situation would have scared me, but his actions seemed perfectly normal. Shock was a terrible thing yet this was so much more. Senna was utterly lost; Adam was the brother he never had. The deceit from Adam was a forgotten memory and the cream pieing from the other month was undoubtedly a way of cheering me up. Yes, Senna and Adam didn't always see eye-to-eye but their bond was undeniable. I couldn't stand in the way of that. I wouldn't.

"Senna…"
He remained bowed in the same position. The only thing to do was join him. Placing my backside down beside his, I felt the instant coldness of the pavement. My pyjama bottoms evidently weren't meant for three am talks on an empty hospital carpark floor. I didn't push him for an answer but instead wrapped my arms around him. It wasn't a proper hug, mainly because my arms were too short, but it hopefully gave him some of the comfort he needed. Silence filled the air and I was soon feeling the coolness of the air a little more than my body appreciated. The hairs on my arms stood tall and I couldn't help but shiver. Senna's body warmth was non-existent but that was the last thing on his mind.

I tried again, "Senna. Come on let's take you home." With that I did my upmost best to lift him up. After the second attempt, he must have felt sorry for my weakness and just let himself be pulled. I waited for him to strap himself in before approaching him again, "Senna you don't have to talk but just give me a sign," and with that he looked at me. I was surprised, not by his sadness, but at his eyes. I'd almost expected them to be red and puffy from crying but instead they seemed the ones of a hollow man. They carried no emotion but then again, the rest of his body told that story with detail. There was no complexity to his emotions, just pure numbness and pain.

The sign was enough, and with that I started the car for the silent journey home. I had no more words to say and for once my automatic counsellor instincts were at a loss. I'd know grief before but this wasn't the usual type. We were mournful over something that hadn't even happened yet. The doctors didn't know Adam like we did. He was a lot of things but a quitter wasn't one of them. I replayed all the times he given up on us, only to come back. If he wanted to live he would yet again maybe he didn't. Maybe he was done with fighting, maybe it wasn't a tragic accident but instead an act of giving up. No matter how hard I tried, I couldn't get the thought out of my head. Had Adam really done this on purpose? I couldn't see him as the attention seeking type.

I turned onto Senna's road to be welcomed by an array of cars. The house opposite Senna's was lit up and people were gathering in the front garden. This was the last thing Senna needed. Pulling over, I turned the engine off. Senna seemed unfazed but remained transfixed on the party that filled his street.

"Do you want me to take you somewhere else?" I didn't expect a reply but asked anyway. He sighed, closed his eyes then spoke, "Not yet" and with that he opened the door, undid his seatbelt then slipped out.

"Sen, where are you going?"

"Sen!" He was storming straight towards the party and was taking no notice of me. I didn't know what was running through his head but surely nothing good could come of this. The man I had picked up less than thirty minutes ago was broken, this man was determined. Following his footsteps, we reached a group of people. Everything was a blur but Senna seemed to know everyone. Shaking a few of their hands, he grabbed himself a drink and cracked it open. Senna needed to let of steam, that was apparent, but everything was so raw I was unsure of this next move.

I was far from in the party mood. My bed and the airport were calling but instead I found myself babysitting a twenty-two-year old man. The time had just ticked five o'clock. Mum and Dad would soon be worrying and I really needed to be getting back. There was no way I was missing this holiday; Adam wouldn't want it. Taking out my phone, I quickly scrolled to Maggie's number and let it dial.

Come on Maggie, come on, pick up the phone!

"Kass…" I knew I'd woken her up but I right now her son needed her.

"Maggie, it's Senna. I picked him up from hospital…" I went on to explain the situation, the position I'd found him in but she didn't seem worried. Something told me that she was only fully aware of how her son acted when he was broken.

"Kass calm down, my boy will be just fine. He got through the last heartache, he'll get through this one. I'll keep a look out. You just get home, haven't you got a plane to catch?" To me, this was worlds apart from a toxic relationship breakup but who was I kidding? I didn't know how Senna had reacted, this girl could have been the one of his dreams.

A plane, yes. I looked towards The Jackson's house to see Maggie standing at her bedroom window. My worry suddenly disappeared. Even under the most intense circumstances Maggie Jackson had that calming influence that just filtered through everyone. Wasn't she even scared? Adam was lying in a coma, with doctors telling us to prefer for the worst. I was a mess and I didn't even like the guy. I wanted to say goodbye to Senna but I had to leave before I got dragged into staying any longer. My phone vibrated in my hand; 'Kass go and get on that plane! And please don't worry about Adam, he's a trooper. We'll ALL see you when you get back. Have a cocktail for me! M and B x.' Her emphasis on 'all' made me instantly smile. I wanted to believe it, I did, but there was a small part of me that could sense something bad was going to happen.

Guilt

Getting off the plane, I knew something was wrong. The overall mood was overcast and even our usual Summer weather seemed worse than usual. We'd only been away two weeks but everything seemed different. I slumped my way through the airport in typical post-holiday blue fashion but this time with a slight sprint; my phone was waiting and I needed to know...

The aftermath of Adam's death was brutal. I didn't know how to feel; contemplating every possible emotion to see if they were justified. I swayed between heartbreak and relief, and in ways saw it as the end to my nightmare, but underneath all my strong persona I was broken. Adam was my first true love, the person that every other guy after he was compared to. He taught me what love was but also the cruel and realistic truth of what heartbreak was. The recent events of the past few months had made me despise him more than usual but that didn't stop me from feeling the same pain as everyone else. A part of me had been torn out; the part that Adam had made. I no longer felt strong but instead weak and ready to break down at any given moment.

The Jackson's were a mess. Bob and Maggie had lost their nephew, the guy they saw more as a second son, and Senna had lost his cousin. It only seemed right for me to keep my distance. My grief seemed unwarranted compared to that of his family. Adam was only a figure of my past; one that I'd been forcing myself to forget ever since his last and final disappearance. I hadn't spoken a nice word about him since, but now all that hatred seemed wrong and undeserved. Memories I had stored away came flooding back and that raw, overwhelming love hit me again.

Downstairs Maggie sat hurled in my mother's arms. Maggie was a stranger; her usual upbeat and smiley body replaced with that of a fragile, pale and broken woman. The pain had added ten years to her complexion. To many her grief seemed extreme but I understood, we all did. It didn't just show the heartbreak of her current loss, but brought back all the grief she still held over the death of her sister. Adam's mum died a year ago and his own death marked the anniversary. The tragedy was unfair in its simplest terms but the way in which he died was a lesson to us all. It was one of those situations where grief had taken another victim. Adam had never properly grieved over his own loss but instead carried on with life, merely saying "it's what Mum would want." A year on and he still hadn't shed a tear in public, he'd alienated his brother and attached himself to a woman, or several. His response was perhaps normal but now it appeared he needed more. He needed someone to make him talk, make him grieve and most of all he needed someone on that doomed day of 3rd August.

I stood in the hallway looking at Maggie and Mum, whilst letting the tears escape from my eyes. Mum cradled her, giving the same motherly affectionate I had become used to. It was true what they said; a mother's hug could fix anything. I stood there watching and longing for one but instead of joining I let Mum comfort someone else for a change. Trying to control my tears, I brushed my eyes with my dressing gown before thinking about getting dressed. It was two in the afternoon, not that it felt it. The past few days had merged into one; our suitcases still occupying the hallway fully packed. It was hard to believe that less than a week ago we were sipping cocktails on a Cancun beach, thinking of anything but Adam lying in a comatose state in hospital. I sighed, causing the tears to fall harder, and ran upstairs before anyone heard me. Now wasn't the time to show weakness.

"Kass?" My head pounded into what I could only see as someone's chest. I didn't look up but instead stared at the floor and cried. I cried hard letting whoever it was embrace me. Their arms wrapped around me tightly; their scent instantly letting me know it was Senna. I wanted to move, struggle out of his firm grip but my body wouldn't let me; it needed this comfort no matter who it was from. I stood there for as long as my legs could hold me before collapsing to the floor with Senna in tow. I hated the thought of him seeing me so weak. It was only a few months ago that I let him throw cream pie over Adam's face because of my hatred. None of this seemed fair.

After what seemed like hours, Senna spoke.

"Kass, come on. Look at me."

His voice was low and whispered. My tears had started to dry up and I knew I couldn't prolong contact for much longer. Truth is I didn't know what to say, how to justify my breakdown. His hand rested under my chin to push my head away from his chest. Gingerly I made eye contact with him. His eyes seemed wider than usual and it was evident he had been crying too; his eyes appearing red and puffy. Once catching my attention he flashed that smile, the one that gave me butterflies after its first viewing; making everything seem normal for just a minute. I was back in The Baggers sitting opposite him; his strong, well-groomed and confident persona drawing me in. I was attached to everything he did, everything he said and soon became needy of him. The tattoo man that sat next to me now was anything but that person; sorrow overshadowed his eyes and showed a weakness that I never thought was possible.

"Kass it'll be ok you know." There he was again, trying to act strong when his body language portrayed anything but. He closed his eyes and sighed. He knew it wouldn't be, I knew it wouldn't be and forcing ourselves to believe it would only be following in Adam's footsteps.
"It has to be;" it sounded like he was trying to reassure himself. I sat with my head against his chest and listened to the sound of his heartbeat. It was slow and seemingly matched the current atmosphere of the house; dull, sad and flat. I closed my eyes trying to think of anything but the past forty-eight hours. Touching back down in England was bad enough without coming back home to this. Senna was soon resting his head on mine.

He'd seen me broken on a number of occasions, the last time being just minutes ago, but now it was my turn to comfort him. Tattoo man was breaking in front of me and all I could do was hold him. His skin was surrounding a completely different person, someone unrecognisable yet it was nice to see his sensitive side. Even under these heart-breaking circumstances, this Senna was the one that touched your heart even more so than his smile. The way I felt towards him now was a different kind of love. It wasn't the jumping butterflies one I felt a few weeks ago but instead the one that felt responsible for getting him out of this slump. He was grieving, just like everyone else in my household but his sorrow was the one effecting me the most.

"Senna, Kass? Are you two…" I turned my head in hope my Dad would get the picture. Now was not the time to be interrupted; not only was I cherishing Senna's need for me but also the silence. The atmosphere was filled was the occasional sniffle but apart from that it was the perfect time for thinking. It was the sweetest sound; the kind of silence that allowed you to take in all the brokenness in the most selfish way possible. I didn't want to hear Adam's name again. He was gone and his shadow that had followed me around for the past year would finally start to fade. There was to be no more comparing other men to him, no more being afraid to fall in love again and no more controlling me from a distance. My nightmare was over. This was the time I could be pleased about all of that; in front of everyone else my eyes would shed the tears they were meant to but for now I needed this. I needed to feel a sense of relief, more for my heart than anything else. Another weight had been lifted off my shoulders. Don't get me wrong, Adam's death would shake everyone's life, mine included, for several months to come. His legacy would remain strong, for we all had something to thank him for and sitting here now that's the only regret I could honestly say I had. I regretted not talking to him one last time; telling him exactly how he made me feel but thanking him at the same time. He'd given me so much hope for something better. Deep down I knew he wasn't a horrible man, just someone who didn't appreciate love for what it really was and for that you couldn't help but feel sorry for him. He'd left this Earth without really experiencing it.

I could hear Dad's footsteps go back down the stairs. Normally I'd welcome my father's comfort but now I had to be the strong one. I had no right to be weak. My strength had to be enough for both mine and Senna's family right now. I told myself my sorrow was based upon guilt and lies; yes, I loved Adam. He was my first true love, the one that I will remember forever, but he gave me so many reasons to hate love; to hate what most people thrive for. I couldn't help but feel guilty; my household was a sombre one with no one knowing what to say to one another yet I knew my life would start to get better. Adam was better staying as a memory rather than a living nightmare and that I had to look forward to, however heartless it sounded.

"Thank you," the sound startled me. I had become so wrapped up in my own state of mind I'd almost forgotten about Senna's. His head was still firmly placed against my chest but his voice seemed to hold less sadness than it had done half an hour ago. I smiled but the reality of the situation was still so raw. Senna clearly wasn't going to be back to his usual self for a while and our friendship, if you could call it that, was one of pure comfort. "What for?" I replied, unsure as to what I'd actually done. Our relationship had drastically changed since my release from hospital. For weeks I'd tried to keep my distance, protect myself from another Adam saga, without listening to what really mattered; my heart. Since Adam, Senna was the first guy to make me smile again and now everything seemed so much clearer. "Being there, Kass. I know how much you hated him." I didn't know what to reply, I could hardly agree with him after the current tragedy. Instead I just squeezed him a bit harder in the hope that he'd take that as a good enough reply. The atmosphere went silence, and just as I thought I'd got away with any more conversation Senna piped up again.

"Kass I don't know what to do now." He didn't really explain himself but he didn't need to; I knew exactly what he meant. His relationship with his cousin was similar to mine with Harrison; being without him would unimaginable. A shiver went down my spine, bringing back the feelings that resulted in my hospital stay. Even the thought of losing Harrison was enough to cause a breakdown let alone losing him for good.

I sat still, staring at my bedroom door ahead, hoping for some words of wisdom to spring to mind; instead I was supplied with nothing. Part of me was done with the morbid mood, however heartless that sounded. Maybe a handshake would put a smile on his face, then again he could think even worse of me. "Kass, are you ok?" This time Senna sat up, leaving an instant cold patch on my chest. He'd had his head lying there for so long I was surprised he hadn't left a dent in my boobs. His eyes seemed brighter and less puffy but his pupils were bigger than ever. For a moment, I kept eye contact, something I'd always been told I struggled with. Staring straight into his eyes, his pain was obvious. He needed, longed, for a response.

"Sen, I'm all good." A small smile crept upon his face. "A smile suits you." I didn't know whether that was the right response, or what he was even smiling about in the first place; still, it gave the atmosphere a brighter buzz. "Sen, Kass? Where did that come from?" Ok, so I couldn't quite tell if he was angry by my automatic nick-naming or whether his smile was genuine. Should I apologise or just roll with it? Luckily, I didn't need to do either. Mum was standing on the stairs peering through the banister; "Hi Mum." Over the past few days she'd been Maggie's rock, similar to the years she'd been mine, but now she looked exhausted. To outsiders it would look as if she had the weight of the world on her shoulders.

"Mum are you ok?"

Her silence worried me but there was no news that could make the situation any worse. Still there was no reply but maybe she just needed an escape. Being a constant crutch to everyone was starting to take its toll and it was horrible to watch. Getting to stand up, I could sense Senna's disapproval but now my Mum needed me and that was more of a priority than he ever would be. I was expecting her to mirror my actions but still she stared straight ahead, clearly zoned out. Instead of pushing it I took my position at the top of the stairs and reached out to her hand. Openly Mum took it but still no movement came.

"Mum just nod, you don't need to say anything," and with that she did. The nod was small and pretty non-existence but it was certainly there. Mum clearly need some alone time so with that I stood up and signalled to Senna that now was the perfect time to cheer up. He seemed reluctant to move, probably because his backside had become mounded to the floor. Goodness knows how long we had been sitting there; all I was certain of was that it was one hell of an emotional experience. After several glares and facial movements, he eventually got the hint; standing up to reveal a very prominent carpet indent. Sliding past Mum on the stairs, I could hear her deep breathing. It sounded so fast yet worn out at the same time. I wanted to reach out to her, just like I had Senna and give her the hug she quite clearly needed but there was something stopping me. Mum's body language was one of anger, hurt and exhaustion, one that was rarely seen. Unsure as to whether an embrace would be accepted or pushed aside, I carried on downstairs, thankfully with Senna in tow. I hated this; hated seeing so many people I cared about hurting. There was nothing I could say to make the situation any better; nothing was bringing Adam back.

In the garden, I found Bob and Dad talking. Even though he was evidently still struggling to contemplate the reality of the disaster, Bob seemed in better spirits. Dad turned round to see Senna and I standing by the back door, "Hey kiddo, you guys ok?" Normally this reaction would have received something like, 'Dad I'm not a kid anymore' for him to only reply 'you'll always be my little girl Kass;' instead I just walked over to him and climbed on his lap. Right now I did feel little; I needed my Dad more than ever. I rested my head on his chest and let him hold me. I was aware that Senna was still hovering in the background, clearly unsure as to where to go and what to say. He could hardly climb on his Dad's lap; I don't think it was have the same effect. With that I sat up, "Bob where's Maggie gone? Is she ok?" Before he could reply Senna walked over and sat in the empty chair, visibly longing to know his Father's answer. Senna's face said it all; he was world's from ok.
"Senna it's ok. Your Mother will be ok. We just need to stick together. Kass she's gone to visit her sister's grave. For some reason she's blaming herself and wanted to apologise for not keeping Adam safe."

It wasn't Maggie's fault. She had given that boy so much love, even after everything he had done. Speaking ill of the dead was something I never agreed with but he'd obviously ruined his cousin's life. Senna was now a broken man, scared of love and now, to add to everything, a grieving mess. I couldn't see him pulling through this, and if he did, the scars he had before would be deeper and harder to fix. The damage was done.

I knew eventually Senna would go back to the non-committal person he was, the person his mother had warned me off so forcefully. He may have been hurting now but in time I only knew too well it would fade. My own grief would seem more bearable and bit by bit I would start to overcome the loss. Adam was a huge part of my life; my first real insight into the male mind, my first heartbreak and more significantly my first love. He had taught me things about relationships that I never knew were true. I learnt more about how not to treat someone than how to but no matter what way you looked at it, they were all valuable life skills.

Grief was a horrible thing. By definition, it was classed as an intense sorrow yet it appeared so much more. It would continue to define us for several months to come. Maggie wouldn't get over Adam's passing like she did her sisters. This time she had no one to be strong for, no one that had to rely on her as heavily as Adam did. Senna would have his father, Bob, my Dad and me, my Mum. Everyone was covered. Running away wasn't her usual style of dealing with things but now it seemed perfectly justified. Maggie could take as long as she wanted and even though it may not have been healthy, it was her way of coping. No judgment could be made.

Part Two
No going back

Love and Hate

Was it possible to love and hate someone at the same time?

Their definition's both surround the concept of strong emotions whilst being on the opposite end of the scale. I was struggling with my emotions, not knowing what I was feeling. Senna had gone cold ever since we lost Adam, either that or I was struggling to accept that he really was just using me. Pushing people away was a conventional sign of grief but it was coming all too familiar as of late. I knew the loss of Adam would follow him around until his own time had come but why he took it out on me was just a prolonged puzzle. Senna had pushed me away ever since Adam's funeral, only giving a toss about me on his watch.

It was now October 2016 and Senna had held a pretty consistent place in my heart for a good fifty-three months, even if his presence lacked. The ups had equalled out the downs, yet I still held him at arm's length to not only protect my heart but protect those around me. It wouldn't just be me that would feel the pain of another heartbreak. In the past four years, I had learnt the meaning of family in its purest form. We were a unit, a unit that carried each other through thick and thin. I owed them everything. The support network from my Mum and Dad was something else. Mum had become used to the odd midnight cry and had happily acted as my comfort blanket to settle the tears. It had been a good seven months since my last heartbreak; a fact I held onto into the hope that things were finally on the up.

Senna was still scared of committing, still useless at contacting when he said he would but I had just accepted that was him. He continued to carry the weight of Adam's death around with him, resulting in him wasting his own life. On numerous occasions, I would remind him of this, telling him that Adam wouldn't want it. Adam needed to live through us, not take us with him. Instead Senna had committed himself to work, more than he had before, and dropped all contact with his parents. They didn't understand him apparently, but truthfully I could see where they were coming from. At a time where they should have been at their strongest, Senna had decided against it.

Maggie and Bob, were still very much present in my life; using the minimal contact I had with their son as proof that he was ok. Every time they asked I yearned to give them more information than him being 'alive'. I thought the term was broad; physically he was here, mentally he was in the past. In time, Maggie had managed to rebuild her broken heart yet her family puzzle remained in pieces. Her pain had become a little less painful and the days a little brighter yet her family jigsaw remained in pieces. It carried no happiness without all the pieces. Her sister and nephew had gone and her son didn't want to know. I believed he did care and honestly thought one of these days he would wake up. To others, my confidence in his feelings towards me could be taken as stupidity or quite simply cockiness. It was neither; I knew how he felt even if he wouldn't admit it to himself. I didn't contact him but instead left the chasing to him. He needed to feel in control and I was more than happy to let him. Instead I used my days to focus on my happiness, my friends and more significantly, my family.

Malia became the most important person in my life. Now grown up, and turning the annoying age of seventeen next month, our relationship had blossomed. We shared style tips and she was often quick in telling me the dos and don'ts from the world's up and coming Vloggers. Apparently, over the knee boots and striped clothing was now a solid trend. She never failed to make me smile at least once a day and her naivety was refreshing, even though slightly frustrating at times. She had no idea of what adult life held for her but was excited nonetheless. There was nothing more satisfying than watching your younger sister grow up into the beautiful and bright young adult she was becoming. That on its own was enough to make me re-evaluate my own life. It would no longer be centred round a boy, and to be more specific, the mysterious tattooed man I'd met all those years ago.

Maggie had stopped warning me off him and had, instead, remained determined to get her boy back. Watching their family fall apart was the hardest thing. The Jackson clan were becoming smaller by the years and Senna didn't seem to care. This side of him was unfair. Fair enough, push me away, but not your mother; she needed him. Her patience was growing thin but she carried on. Maggie was one of the most stubborn people I knew, apart from myself. I remained optimistic; I had no other choice. One of these days he had to see sense.

Looking back now, I was sadly and illogically fixated with every movement Senna made. I was drawn in by the simplest of things, the most ironic messages and nothing anyone said would change it. Blinded by his smile, I became guilty of being someone I usually pitied; someone controlled. Senna didn't control me, but my feelings towards him did. My friends had got sick to death of my fantasy and had reverted to letting me get on with it, 'Kass, it'll end in disaster but we trust you.' It was all lies; they didn't trust me at all and they had every right not to. I had gone from being the sanest person out of the four us to the craziest in the space of one boy.

Like any other young adult, I still had dreams; dreams that to everyone else were running out of time, to me they were very much still on track. They weren't going to be as easy as I first planned but they would happen, if it was the last thing I did. It was after Adam's death that I knew Senna would be a part of them, I just didn't know what part he'd play until now. I had gone through months of accepting that Senna and I would remain as just friends. I would be his support network when he missed his cousin but would also embrace the quiet times; the times that he did his disappearing act. He'd never really given me full reign to see other people but as we were never theoretically together he could only sit back, watch and dislike it. If only I had had the same mentality a few years back, my heart would have received a lot less of a beating.

Putting a label on what Senna and I was an impossible task. Friends? Yes. More than friends? Yes, but lovers? No. To him, 'it was the way it had to be.' Apparently, the risk of him hurting me was too high. In a way, I had to thank him for trying to protect me. On the other hand, I felt crushed every time he said it. This feeling had become very much part of my makeup, becoming a professional at hiding it. The panic attacks of years back were long behind me and the bullets he delivered felt more like a pin pricks. My heart had slowly but surely rebuilt itself. I would often joke around with him, asking if he had something he had to tell me. Each time he ensured me there was nothing else and that he really was just trying to do the right thing. If it wasn't for his endless flirtatious banter I would have accepted friends just like that.

Maybe it was a cruel joke; maybe Senna did deliberately mean to string me along but I didn't have the strength to question it. Over the past four years I had fallen out with him more times than I could physically remember. I would go through weeks of not talking to him, for him only to pop back up and mess with my head again; each time I would stupidly let him. My willpower was weak and my feelings were strong. The balance was all wrong and there was only going to be one winner. I wasn't ashamed or afraid to admit I loved him. The problem was explaining why. On paper, Senna was right up there with Adam; a waste of space as a romantic partner. In real life, he had surprised me in more ways than I thought was humanly possible. He had taught me things about myself that I could only dream of being true. I was stronger than I thought, I had more confidence than I thought and I was worth so much more than second best.

Losing Adam was painful at the easiest of times. I needed both Senna and Adam in my life and after losing one I knew I couldn't lose the other. Senna had promised me a meal for my birthday and for once he seemed to be following through with a promise. It was the sixteenth, three days before I turned twenty-three. Up until the exact hour I was prepared for further disappointment; for Senna to cancel as per usual. He never did. The meal was textbook date material; a candlelit table for two, a bottle of wine (or two) and impeccable food. He'd managed to put his snobby food requests aside for me and for the first time since Adam died I felt special to him. Senna didn't see me as Adam's ex but instead as Kassia Green, the girl he met all those years ago. I longed for him to offer more, needed him to give me more. Our stories were worlds apart and I was struggling to find the same page as him. His novel consisted of no romance whereas my fairytale ending was looking further and further away the longer Senna stayed in my life.

Adam had become part of my make-up and I truly believed he was watching every step I took. I found myself promising him I would look after Senna, hoping that it would make up for not being there for him. Numerous times I wanted to walk away, wanted to tell him we were done and that there was nothing he could say to change it. My heart had open-heartedly taken a beating, one that I didn't know the cure for. Senna was both the medicine and the reason. I guess I was hoping for a miracle, a sign, to tell me what to do. Ever since the textbooks had been taken away from me at school, I had struggled. I struggled with making decisions that stuck, decisions that were sensible and decisions that were smart. I'd gone from a bright kid to a useless adult.

Playlist

That meal was the last one we had; the last time I saw him…

My usual upbeat playlist now consisted of nothing but love songs; all of which made sense. Without even meaning to they were as poignant as they got. They were the kind of songs that every heartbroken person could relate to; covering topics such as 'how to love again' and 'being yourself'. No matter what angle you took them from, they were the perfect way of realising you were not alone. I knew I wasn't the only one that had experienced heartbreak, I knew I wasn't the first person to feel alone but what I did know was that I would be ok. No one was worth the number of tears I had shed over the past four years. Not even Tattoo Man.

It was in that moment that my decision was solidified; letting go was the only option. This time was different though, there was to be no brief declutter but instead a complete cleanse. Tattoo Man was to be a figure of my past rather than my future. Adam was not to be mentioned at all; only thought about on the fifteen of every August. Between the pair of them my heart had received a beating, so much so that I was surprised it was still working. They'd been trips to hospital, several crying breakdowns and five years of thinking I really was not good enough. I wouldn't have got through it without my family and for that I will be forever grateful. Not just that, but I was physically and mentally tired. The past five years had seen every emotion possible; from heartbreak to excitement, tiredness to joy and pure sadness to overwhelming happiness. In ways Senna and Adam were to both blame and thank. They'd given me some of the best laughs yet been the reason for many tears.

The hardest part to accept was the missed opportunities. Over the past four years my friendship group had expanded; Lukas had come into my life bringing his own issues that gave me something else to focus on. People would ask, "Kass, do you not just want a simple life?" Truth is, it was all I longed for but there was something about being there for other people. Whether it was part of me blaming myself for not making Adam talk, or whether it was down to pure denial of my own heartbreak, was just something that I needed to figure out. Either way, my friends and family needed me now; Harry, Kieran, Nate and now Lukas would get me through I just needed a little faith. Lukas reminded me of Adam in so many ways; his blonde hair and blue eyes instantly making him special. I didn't want to compare him to Adam but I couldn't help it. I knew he'd be special but that was a story for another day.

Senna was going. There was to be no more late night calls for comfort, no more using me to make him feel good about himself. He was running away, just like his Mother said he would, but this time was different. It wasn't because he was scared but instead an act of selfishness. Before leaving he'd thanked me for seeing the best in him when no one else did. If anything, I felt stupid, felt stupid for believing his words. Everyone else had seen his true colours where I hadn't. From Harrison to Nate, Kieran to his own Mother, I had been told numerous times to let him go. Instead I held onto him, scared of not having him in my life.

Over the years, I had convinced myself that I could change him; mold him into the perfect man. Truth was that he was happy. He was happy alone, happy putting his job before everything and everyone else, so much so that even his Mother had given up on him. Looking back now I should have read the signs; should have known that however understanding I was it would never be good enough. I can squirm at the times I begged for time and attention. Not only had he hurt me but he'd made me look stupid. He'd happily slept around, and supposedly been in a relationship with someone else, if that's what you could call it. It wasn't a relationship, she just gave him what he needed, however crude that sounded. I remember my heart feeling cheated and his response being "but we're not together, never have been and never will be." To anyone else that should have been enough to cut the rope; I, instead, went on a mind game of figuring out what I had done wrong.

To a young girl, those words hurt. Love is a nasty thing. It took me the first few years to realise how I felt about him, understand why I couldn't walk away. I didn't want to love Senna, I just couldn't help myself. I tried convincing myself it was because of his tie to Adam but Adam had now been gone for three years and the feelings were still the same. Sadly, it wasn't Adam; I was just totally and utterly in love with Senna however much I tried to fight it. As far as men came, Senna was the worst. He didn't just make you love him but he then used it to his advantage. I went through the heartache avoidance routine on multiple occasions; blocking his number, deleting him on Facebook, to only undo it to see if he actually cared. Each time I'd come back to find a message, the usual ones being 'I miss you' or 'I'm sorry.' I was only too familiar with these messages, mainly from my ups and downs with Adam. It got me believing that every guy was the same; that they all had the same game plan.

Don't get me wrong I knew Senna cared. I knew he longed to be able to commit but he was clearly just damaged. Even his leaving wasn't as simple as it should have been. A few days before he left, I received a message declaring everything I had always longed to hear:

"Kass, I need to say thank you. Thank you for everything you've done. You never gave up on me when everyone else did. I didn't realise what I felt and I'm sorry. I now know I love you. I love you whole-heartedly and will be forever thankful for everything. Adam was right, you are special. Senna x"

It was everything I had wanted to hear for so long but I couldn't help but feel disappointed. There wasn't the butterflies I had expected but instead an empty hole. I felt numb. He had already told me he was leaving (running away) so what was the point in telling me how he felt? Part of me thought he was playing with me one last time, the other part of me believed it.

Even though, now twenty-three, I still felt the same as I did all those years ago, when Adam had left. I still found it hard to explain my emotions, to block out the negativity and focus on the positives. Right now, I could see no good in any of this. Through the Jackson family I had lost two people; one ending in the worst possible way, the other in simply a coward attempt of avoiding commitment. Something told me our story wasn't over but for now this chapter certainly was. There was no point in getting upset, no point in begging him to stay. I'd never seen Senna as a nightmare before but maybe he was. Maybe now I could move on. Maybe he was doing me a favour.

Tears would continue to fill my eyes but would fail to fall. Maybe the tears had finally run out…

Kassia's Playlist

After heartbreak, some people turn to drugs, others drink but for me it was music. There was something about the lyrics that made all my feelings seem worthy, seem normal. There was no handbook on how to feel, no one telling me the next steps to make but instead someone that you could relate to. Sharing a story as personal as this was nothing to be ashamed of. It had taken two shattered hearts and a thousand soggy tissues for me to realize that I had never been alone. I became to realize that heartbreak, channeled in the right way, could bring some good.

Musicians wrote music, I wrote my story...

Tell Your Heart to Beat Again
Danny Gokey

You're shattered
Like you've never been before
The life you knew
In a thousand pieces on the floor
And words fall short in times like these
When this world drives you to your knees
You think you're never gonna get back
To the you that used to be

Tell your heart to beat again
Close your eyes and breathe it in
Let the shadows fall away
Step into the light of grace
Yesterday's a closing door
You don't live there anymore
Say goodbye to where you've been
And tell your heart to beat again

Beginning
Just let that word wash over you
It's alright now
Love's healing hands have pulled you through
So get back up, take step one
Leave the darkness, feel the sun
'Cause your story's far from over
And your journey's just begun

Tell your heart to beat again
Close your eyes and breathe it in

Let the shadows fall away
Step into the light of grace
Yesterday's a closing door
You don't live there anymore
Say goodbye to where you've been
And tell your heart to beat again

Let every heartbreak
And every scar
Be a picture that reminds you
Who has carried you this far
'Cause love sees farther than you ever could
In this moment heaven's working
Everything for your good

Tell your heart to beat again
Close your eyes and breathe it in
Let the shadows fall away
Step into the light of grace
Yesterday's a closing door
You don't live there anymore
Say goodbye to where you've been
And tell your heart to beat again
Your heart to beat again
Beat again

Oh, so tell your heart to beat again

Ready to be Myself
David Dun

Today, today is the day
I'm waking up to say
I'm tired of the way
The way that I change
I rearrange Myself to be
Someone that everybody loves
So I become someone I'm not

Who am I gonna be
When no body's watching me
I want to be real
What am I gonna do
To live what I know is true
I let go
Oh I've been someone else
God I'm ready to be myself

Now, now is the time
To open up my eyes
And see what I will find
I find I
Made up my mind
To be someone that everybody loves
So I became someone I'm not

Who am I gonna be
When no body's watching me
I want to be real
What am I gonna do

To *live what I know is true*
I let go
Oh I've been someone else
God I'm ready to be myself

I want to be something more
Then a man who needs to be adored
It shouldn't matter to me
And with every breath that I have left
I wanna breath it out hoping that
He says "you've done well"

Who am I gonna be
What am I gonna do

Who am I gonna be
When no body's watching me
I want to be real
What am I gonna do
To live what I know is true
I let go
Oh I've been someone else
God I'm ready to be myself

Oh I've been someone
Oh I've been someone
Oh I've been someone else
I'm ready to be myself
God I'm ready to be myself

Save Myself
Ed Sheeran

I gave all my oxygen to people that could breathe
I gave away my money and now we don't even speak
I drove miles and miles, but would you do the same for me?
Oh, honestly?
Offered off my shoulder just for you to cry upon
Gave you constant shelter and a bed to keep you warm
They gave me the heartache and in return I gave a song
It goes on and on

Life can get you down so I just numb the way it feels
I drown it with a drink and out-of-date prescription pills
And all the ones that love me they just left me on the shelf
No farewell
So before I save someone else, I've got to save myself

I gave you all my energy and I took away your pain
'Cause human beings are destined to radiate or dream
What line do we stand upon 'cause from here looks the same?
And only scars remain
Life can get you down so I just numb the way it feels
I drown it with a drink and out-of-date prescription pills
And all the ones that love me they just left me on the shelf
No farewell
So before I save someone else, I've got to save myself

But if don't
Then I'll go back
To where I'm rescuing a stranger

187

Just because they needed saving just like that
Oh, I'm here again
Between the devil and the danger
But I guess it's just my nature
My dad was wrong
'Cause I'm not like my mum
'Cause she'd just smile and I'm complaining in a song
But it helps
So before I save someone else
I've got to save myself

Life can get you down so I just numb the way it feels
I drown it with a drink and out-of-date prescription pills
And all the ones that love me they just left me on the shelf
No farewell
So before I save someone else, I've got to save myself
And before I blame someone else, I've got to save myself
And before I love someone else, I've got to love myself

Printed in Great Britain
by Amazon